I0594707

the Weaving

Rochelle McDonnell

Copyrights

Originally published in 2016 by Jewel House, Perth, Western Australia,
in eBook ISBN 978-0-9943564-4-4

Copyright © 2016 R. McDonnell.

The moral right of Rochelle McDonnell to be asserted as the author of this work
has been asserted in accordance with the Australian Copyright Law
as set out in the Copyright Act 1968 (Cth).
This is federal legislation, and applies throughout Australia.

All Rights reserved, no part of this publication may be reproduced or transmitted
in any formby any means, electronic or mechanical, including photocopy,
recording or any information storage and retrieval system,
without permission in writing from the Publisher, except for the use of
brief quotations in a book review.

This book is a work of fiction. Names, Characters, Businesses, Organisations,
Places and Events are either the product of the author's imagination or are
used fictitiously. Any resemblance to actual persons, living or dead, events or
locales is entirely coincidental.

National Library of Australia Cataloguing-in Publication Data,
catalogue record for this book is available on request from the
National Library of Australia

ISBN Number: 978-0-6484481-5-0 - ePub

PICARDIC PRESS
PUBLISHING

the Weaving

arkness surrounded her. Moving slowly, feeling for the firmness of the hewn rock, her hand slid down the golden rail. She stepped carefully, the dragon dancing and weaving beside her. His breath warm, his presence comforting, she turned to him, waiting for guidance.

He shrugged and hovered over her hand, the emerald green of his scales glittered in the muted light. His eyes red and piercing held hers before he settled on her shoulder.

"Where to now?" she whispered.

"I cannot tell, I cannot say, only you have knowledge of the way," he sang.

Resting her hand on the wall, she took another step into the dark room. Hidden lamps glowed softly, casting shadows over the tapestries that lined a long corridor. Stepping back in surprise, she peered around the corner as the darkness chased the fading light.

Thrown into darkness again, she sighed. The lamps glowed dimly, and then flared with light. Stepping back, she watched them fade and the darkness wrap around her.

Giggling with delight, she jumped onto the floor. The lights glowed soft and comforting, like the kiss of the moon, caressing all it touches.

"Which way?" she whispered.

"I cannot say, I cannot show, you alone know which way to go," he sang.

Her fingers to rest upon the delicate weave, she stretched out her hand.

Afraid to take the next step, she dropped her hand in surprise when the tapestry curled away from her.

"This be the beginning, the weaving of what is, the touch of what is to come," the tapestry softly sang.

Leaping from her shoulder, the dragon fluttered before the woven beauty, its wings gently fanning the golden threads. The threads began to unravel, curling into tiny golden balls, each hanging from the tapestry and swaying gently in the breeze created by the dragon's wings.

Then, if by an unseen hand, it began to recreate. Tiny balls of gold became a dirty brown, the brilliant reds faded to a rusty glow. The brilliance and beauty of colour faded, as the golden threads moved through the tapestry.

"Why?" she whispered.

"Your hand has not created, the threads are not yet yours to place," the dragon sang softly.

"What must I do?"

"That I cannot say, nor can I tell, when it is time, you must pick the thread and weave it well."

Fingers trembling, she reached for a golden strand. It appeared to have no place in the picture, no function of its own. A single thread, small and delicate, tightly curled. She gently prised it from the tapestry.

Holding it between her fingers, she gazed upon its beauty.

Laying it in the palm of her hand, she caressed the fine thread. Warming to her touch, it glowed. The single strands, tightened, bonding together, as if the hand of an unseen weaver worked it to strength.

"What do I do?"

"It is not for me to tell, or to show, place the thread where it must go," the dragon sang.

Stepping back, she looked at the tapestry awash with colours of the earth, deep rusts and the brownest of brown. The golden beauty of the single thread seemed to have no place. Its splendour and strength, foreign to the weave before her.

"Now," the tapestry whispered.

The threads began to move and dance under her touch. Placing the end against the rusty red, it shivered in her fingers, then moved quickly, flowing freely amongst the threads of rust.

"Wait," it whispered.

Her eyes fixed on the golden thread, she watched if grow, spreading its warmth, drawing the earthen colours into itself, changing them to the most vibrant browns, the deepest reds, the greenest greens.

The tapestry moved and breathed, drawing life from the single strand. The brown became the strongest root of a tree, the red the wildflowers that grew beneath, the greens folded and bent into the shiniest of leaves. The golden thread settled amongst the red flowers, moving and shimmering, weaving and swaying. The lamp above the tapestry flared and glowed brightly.

Shading her eyes with her hand, she waited.

The tapestry shimmered. Red flowers morphed into the richest of gowns, joining together with the golden thread, and then, draping around the slender brown trunk, embracing it fully. The leaves danced and laughed, turning a golden hue.

"Close your eyes," the dragon whispered.

Slowly lowering her eyelids, she did as she was told.

The sound of rustling filled her ears. Squeezing her eyes tightly closed, she willed herself not to open them. She felt the soft breath of another move across her face, and then, the sound of a footfall. A muffled sound, amplified by the silence, caressed the stone walls, and gently teased her curiosity.

"Eyes you may open," he sang.

Afraid, she breathed deeply and then, slowly opened her eyes.

Before her stood the fairest maiden. Her hair golden, her eyes blue as the rarest gem, the red gown draped, and folded around her.

"Welcome… now our journey begins."

Confused and surprised she stared at the young woman before her. "I don't understand."

"This is the beginning of understanding. I am called Celeste, what are you known by?"

She turned to the dragon. He shrugged and fluttered over Celeste.

"Your name I cannot say, nor can I show the way," he sang.

"Choose carefully the name that you will wear, for when it is spoken, all will hear," Celeste said softly.

Fear, greater than the mystical curiosity that tickled her mind, pulled her toward the steps.

"Wait...it is not time to leave...It is time to weave," the dragon sang.

Celeste held out her hand and waited, her face soft, her eyes calling to her. Raising her hand slowly, she placed it gently in Celeste's.

The warmth of her touch stilled the fear. An awakening deep within yawned and groaned. She felt a yearning to move closer, yet she remained still.

"Come," Celeste encouraged.

She stepped toward the door hidden behind the tapestry.

"Open it," she whispered.

"I have no key."

Celeste smiled, "You are the key."

She touched it gently, pulling her hand back in surprise when it pulsed with the beat of her heart.

"Wait," Celeste said quietly.

Lifting her gown, she pulled on the deep red thread that hung from the hem. Tugging gently, she wrapped the red cord around her fingers.

"Give me your hand."

Tying the cord around the girl's wrist, she knotted it carefully.

"Now you may enter," Celeste whispered.

"I don't understand," she said, looking at the dragon.

"I cannot tell, I cannot show, through the door you must go," he sang.

*P*ushing gently, she waited for the door to move. The solid timbers roughly hewn, stood fast. She moved her hand, searching for the handle, her eyes fixed on the knotted wood.

Sighing, she leaned heavily against the door. The wood groaned and breathed, resonating with the beat of her heart. She felt a movement, a slight give in the firmness, a shimmering which pulsed with life. She looked around for Celeste, and saw only the dim shadows of light.

"Who doth enter my chamber?"

Turning in surprise she looked for the voice, peering into the shadows of light and dark, straining to see.

"Well, speak child."

"Who are you," she whispered.

The room filled with laughter, she moved slowly towards the sound.

"That be thy question?" the voice asked. "Surely thee seeks more than the name I wear… is not your mind filled with wonder?"

"Where are you?"

"I stand before thee, rely not only on thy sight."

"I don't understand," she whispered, touching the red cord tied tightly to her wrist.

"The speaking of truth is part of the seeing. Move thy feet child. Move toward me that I may truly see thee."

"How can I move to you when I don't know where you are?"

"Then walk in the darkness, trust thy steps."

"But…"

"Silence, listen to all that is and all that could be… open thine ears to hear what cannot be seen with thine eyes… reach out with the inner eye of self."

She moved slowly, taking small uncertain steps toward the voice that beckoned her.

"Thou doest well," the voice whispered.

She stopped and turned. Listening, opening herself to the darkness, searching for the voice.

"Sit," the voice said.

Groping in the darkness, she felt for the chair.

"Trust that it will be… sit," the voice encouraged.

"But…"

"Hush child, now sit."

Bending her knees, her eyes closed, she lowered herself slowly. Surprised to find the firmness of a stool against her legs, she sat.

"The first test thou hast past, well done child," the voice said softly.

Peering into the flickering shadows, she searched for the one who spoke.

"Now, let us move to the second…say to me of this room, tell me what thine eyes perceive."

"Nothing, I see nothing," she whispered.

"Then thou hast not looked," the voice said softly.

"I am looking," she snapped.

"Ahhh, the fire of injustice doth begin to burn in thee."

Sighing deeply, she touched the red cord around her wrist, turned on the stool and willed her eyes to see through the shadows.

"Comfort thee finds in the touching of the cord?"

"Yes."

"It is only a cord, what comfort doth it bring?"

"I don't know," she whispered.

"Nay, thou dost not."

"I don't understand."

A gentle hand rested on her shoulder. She turned quickly.

"Child, still thy fear and harness thy tongue. This be the beginning of the weaving, the quest which thou hast sought, yet thee quarrels with self. The seeking of understanding is not by way of words."

She looked down at the hand resting on her shoulder. Aged and frail, veins pulsing with life, the hand was strong and the warmth comforting.

"Now child, be upstanding and take my hand in thine."

Standing slowly, she reached behind to move the stool. Surprise and fear tickled when she realised there was no stool.

"Fear not. Walk with me, trust thy steps, and be diligent to the words spoken. The quest thou hast sought be one fraught with many dangers, to be equipped is wisdom."

Placing her hand on the one resting on her shoulder she lifted it gently, and entwined her fingers with the unseen voice.

"It is so dark," the girl whispered.

"There be no light, but this doth not mean there is only darkness. Tis foolishness to rely on thine eyes alone," the voice replied, as they walked together. "Once thou hast moved from here to there, for now thou art betwixt and between, thee will do well to remember this. The way will not always be clear to thee, thy steps will be uncertain. Even though the sun doth rise and the moon doth shine, darkness will dance with thee."

Unsure of her steps, the child broke her stride, searching for the face of the one whose hand she held.

"Where are we?" she asked.

"We be where we need to be… Child, hast thou taken heed of the words spoken to thee, nay, I think not. Fear doth gnaw at thee. It be like a dog with a bone, cracking and breaking to suck the marrow of life....thou must master the fear or it will take from thee the life sought."

Sighing deeply, she turned toward the voice. "Why can't I see you?"

"Tis what thee wishes?"

"Yes," she whispered.

"Perchance thou could see, then what? Will thy curiosity be sated,

will thy thoughts be stilled, thy tongue bridled so thee can learn what must be taught?" The words gentle, bathed the child with uncertainty.

"Maybe," she said quietly.

"Child, thou hast much to learn and the time be short, yet thee still wrestles with self...why choose the quest if thou doth not wish to learn the weaving?"

lutching tightly to the hand that held hers, she waited, stilling her mind.

"Good thy thoughts are calm…sit child, and I will tell thee what thou seeks to know,"

Groping in the darkness she felt for a chair, a stool, anything to sit on.

"On the ground, child." The voice was soft and comforting. "Sit on the ground, and let thy feet dangle in the brook, feel its coolness while I speak to thee."

Cautiously she bent her knees and lowered herself to the ground. She felt the soft tickle of grass on her hand and the give of the earth as she sat. Listening for the sound of running water, she waited, and then stretched out her feet. The coolness of the water surprised her, as did the gentleness of its touch.

"Well done child… Now, the weaving be the strengthening of all things, the binding to thy self all that must be bound, so thy quest be one of honour. Tis the understanding of what is and what is not, the seeing beyond seeing, the knowing beyond knowing. Tis the breath which feeds thee, and the same breath which takes from thee."

The child sat in silence listening to the one who spoke, uncurling the words and searching for their meaning.

"Thou hast understanding?"

Shaking her head and wiggling her toes in the water, she turned toward the voice. "No," the child whispered.

"Nay… yet thee sits with thy feet in water …does the water be there?"

"Yes, I can feel it and the grass as well."

"Aye, yet thine eyes do not see. That be the weaving child, that be the weaving."

"So it is, because I expected it to be there?" she asked with caution.

"There be some truth in thy answer," the voice said kindly. "Alas, it only be some."

"Oh," she breathed, laying back on the grass she peered into the darkness. "Some truth is better than none though, right?"

"Nay child it be not," she said gently.

"It be not," she whispered.

"Aye," the voice confirmed. "Tell me what thine eye sees as thee gazes above?"

She turned toward the voice, hoping for a glimpse of the face.

"Above thee I did ask," the voice encouraged.

Giggling, she turned away and gazed above her, willing to see past the darkness.

"I see shadows, grey and murky, moving and melting into each other," she said softly.

"Reach beyond the shadows."

"I see more shadows," she said playfully.

A hand rested gently on her head. "Child, twill be time for games on the morrow, this be time for learning."

"Sorry," she whispered.

"Thou art not sorrowful child, thy heart dances with excitement, and mischief is afoot in thy mind."

"A little, but not too much mischief," the child teased.

"Tis good fear is harnessed," the voice said softly, "now reach beyond the shadows and tell me what is seen."

They sat in silence as she willed her eyes to look beyond the shadows.

"I see something," she whispered.

"Say to me of this something."

"Well it's like a different shadow, softer and there is some colour to it."

"Aye, continue thy search."

"Continue thy search," she whispered.

"Dost thou mock my words?"

"No."

"Dost thou seek acceptance through mimicry?"

"No," she whispered.

"Then bridle thy tongue and do what has been asked of thee."

"I'm sorry," she said quietly.

"For one who doth know little, thou seems to have much sorrow."

"I am not sad, if that's what you mean," she challenged. Tired of the confusion and the expectation, she sat up and rested on her hands.

"Child, rebellion doth not wear well with thee. When one doth to say thou art sorry, it doth mean their heart be heavy with sorrow for the speaking of harm or the deed which has caused harm. That sorrow I do not see in thee, thou would do well to remember these words on thy quest."

The words carried on waves of gentleness, softened the rebuke and allowed it to settle comfortably with the child.

Breathing deeply, she searched through the shadows, catching a glimpse of the face which looked intently at her.

"Now child, stand and walk to the lea and bring to me the stinging nettle and the flower of chamomile."

"What lea?"

"The one before thee. Now, stand child and walk the land, harvest what be asked of thee."

"There is no field," she snapped.

"Then sit child, and wait until thee sees."

Fingering the cord around her wrist, she felt for the strand that attached her to Celeste.

"Thou hast thoughts of following the cord?"

"Maybe," she said, frustration edging the word.

"Maybe? Child, the cord follows it does not to lead," the voice told her.

"That doesn't make any sense, if it follows me then I can follow it back."

"So thou sayest," the voice whispered.

Sighing deeply, the girl stood and peered into the shadows before her.

"The harvest be thy task. The longer thee tarries greater the burden of the harvest."

She turned toward the voice. "I have no idea what I'm looking for."

"Twill be an interesting harvest."

Taking a step forward, the girl swallowed back the anger.

"If thou be equipped with scales and gills, take the next step, if not, find another way," the voice said gently.

Sighing deeply, she turned and walked along the bank of the brook.

"Thou hast made a wise choice," the voice called after her.

"So pleased," she whispered. "Think about the field, see the nettles, find the way over the brook," she said quietly, finding comfort in the sound of her voice.

ippling greens moved under her feet, and the shadows began to take form. Standing still she breathed deeply, amazed by the twisted trunk of a tree rising before her.

The smile moved freely and settled as the fields of yellows and reds opened before her. The air was fragrant with perfumes, delicate and true, blending and melding together, each note soaring and supporting the one beneath.

Laughing, she ran through the flowers, throwing herself to the ground and burrowing into the deep greens of their stems. The blueness of the sky, gentle and caressing, moved silently, bringing into focus each petal and stamen dancing in the soft breeze.

Awakened to the urgency of her task, she pushed up from the ground and closed her eyes.

"Nettles," she whispered.

A dark green patch of plants caught her eye. Running toward them, she reached to pluck the tender shoots. Pain, burning and deep, scaled her fingers.

Pulling back in surprise, she looked down at her hands. Reaching in again she touched the dark green leaves, the stinging sensation crept through her fingers and ran up her arms.

"Great," she whispered, shaking her hands in the vain attempt to stop the burning.

Gathering up her skirt and wrapping it around her hand, she plucked the tender leaves. Working quickly, she gathered them into her skirt. Stepping away from the patch, she moved toward the white flowers of the chamomile.

Snapping the heads, she laid them on top of the nettles. Her skirt full, she held it tightly as she made her way through the fields and back to the brook.

She followed the swirling wood smoke which caressed the sky with delicate strokes of grey and white. The woman was bent over the fire, encouraging the hot coals. Smiling, the woman looked up at the child. Her face, soft and welcoming, eyes dark and beckoning, her hair a deep auburn colour falling freely around her. The shawl, the richest purple, her gown, a deeper purple speckled with sliver thread.

"Child."

"Hello," she whispered, taken aback by her beauty.

"Thou hast found what was asked of thee?"

"Yes," she said, taking a small step closer to the woman.

"Thou hast done well, lay thy harvest down."

Letting go of the ends of her skirt, the nettles and chamomile fell softly to the ground. "Now I can make wine."

"We are going to make wine?"

"Nay, I am making wine."

"But the nettles sting and burn," she said, holding up her hands.

"Aye they do, come sit," she said, patting the ground next to her. The woman knelt down next to the nettles and flowers. Plucking several chamomile heads, cautious not to touch the nettles, she placed them in a cloth and tied it firmly.

Resting the bundle on a rock, she gently rolled another over the bundle. Moving to the fire she lifted the pot and carried it carefully. Holding the cloth by the edge she dipped it into the warm water.

"Hold out thy hands," she said, sitting next to the girl. "Twill ease the sting." She placed the small bundle in the girl's hands. "Press down to release the oil."

"Thank you."

The woman held her gaze before tending to the fire. Brushing the hot coals to the side of the stones, she added another piece of wood.

"You didn't need nettles did you?"

"Yet thee harvested what was not needed," she said softly, turning to look at her.

"Why?" the girl asked, pressing down on the poultice and releasing the oil.

"To see if thou be willing to touch that which would cause thee pain," she said quietly. "To soil thy garment, to walk in a place unknown, to seek out that which thou knowest not, this be part of the weaving."

Looking down at the green and yellow stains on her skirt and the soil which still clung to it, she sighed. Lifting the poultice she looked at her hand, each finger red and pulsing with pain. Laying her hand back on the poultice she worked it with her fingers, the oil from the chamomile gentle and soothing.

"And if I hadn't brought you the nettles?"

"Then another task would have been set for thee."

"Another task?" she whispered, squeezing the poultice.

"Aye." The woman turned to look at the girl. "Perchance the danger be greater, the pain deeper, the task a greater challenge than the one set for thee."

"What was the point of gathering the nettles, I truly don't understand."

"Child, child," she whispered, moving closer to her. "Thou didst what was bidden without question…perchance a question would have helped thee avoid the pain of the nettles sting."

"But you said understanding is not by way of words," she challenged.

"This be truth, understanding be found in completing the task, knowledge, by the gathering of words… now thee has both."

Stepping on her skirt, she looked down at the tear. Frustrated, she sat on the edge of the rock and looked to Celeste.

"How much further?"

Shrugging, Celeste looked up at the ragged steps and then back at the girl.

"We are far from where we need to be," she said.

Lifting her skirt, she tugged at the rip, then pulled against the weft of the cloth. Tearing off a long strip, she stood slowly and looked down at her feet. Draping the torn piece of skirt around her neck, she knotted it and smiled up at Celeste.

"Okay, let's go," the girl said with a tinge of shyness.

Lightening slashed the sky and danced through the darkness. Waiting for the thunder clap, she stood with her hands on her hips, and looked up at the path before her.

"Why are we doing this?" She turned to Celeste, her look challenging.

"Why?"

"It must be done," Celeste replied.

"It must be done?"

"Have you not learned anything?" Celeste asked.

"Apparently not," she answered, placing her foot on the broken rock, her hand on the bent knee, she pushed down as she took another step.

"Now is not the time for questions, it is the time for climbing," Celeste told her as they climbed together.

"Will there be a time for questions?"

"Yes there will be time for questions, each one must be asked with thought and care."

Fingering the red cord around her wrist she looked down at Celeste's gown.

"Why does the cord seem shorter?"

"Because it is," she said with a smile, "and when it needs to be longer, it will be."

Tired and confused the child sat on the edge of a rock and rested her head in her hands.

"We must continue," Celeste encouraged her.

She shook her head. "No…Not until you tell me where we are going and why."

"Then you will be sitting here for a long time." She started to climb. "I suggest you follow me. To be alone when the sun has set, be not wisdom."

"The sun has already set, it's dark and cold, and there is a storm coming."

"True, so heed my words," she called over her shoulder.

Sighing, she rested her finger tips on the cold stone above her head.

"Stop," Celeste yelled. "Don't move."

Flushed with fear, she began to lift her fingers from the rock.

"Don't move," Celeste whispered. "Keep your fingers where they are, stay still."

Turning to look at Celeste, she felt a cold prickling sensation on her fingers.

"It has begun," Celeste said softly. "Close your eyes and remain still, no matter what you hear, what you feel, remain still and keep your eyes closed."

"Why?" she whispered.

"Do as I say and do it now or it will consume you."

Held rigid with fear and uncertainty, she closed her eyes. Her fingers burned, cold and hot. Pain fierce and crippling clawed at her hand. Willing herself to stand still, she began to shake, the pain strangling and demanding.

"Still, very still, empty your mind of all thoughts, do not move," Celeste whispered.

A small sob escaped through clenched teeth, her mouth filled with a scream that could not escape.

"Hold your breath, do not move," Celeste whispered.

Focusing on the red cord around her wrist, she held her breath fighting the pain and the bitter taste in her mouth.

Her wrist began to quiver, the cord burned like fire, tiny drops of blood fell to the ground as the cord cut deeper.

"Focus on nothing, empty your mind," Celeste reminded her.

Unconsciously she took a small step.

"No," Celeste breathed. "No, still child, very still."

A roaring sound filled her ears. Pressing her eyelids tightly shut she tried to hang on, to stay still, to focus on nothing. Her arm ached from being raised above her head, her fingers burned with pain, she craved for air.

"It is almost over," Celeste whispered.

Her feet felt heavy and seemed to be pressing into the hard rock. Waves of dizziness assaulted her. Unable to stand any longer, she fell to the ground.

ossing on the straw filled mattress, her mind filled with images, the child lay bound in restlessness.

Her hand resting gently on the child's head, Celeste looked over at the woman.

"It did not go well I see," the woman stated.

"No, the poison runs strongly."

Sighing deeply, she stirred the small pot over the fire.

"The challenge still waits," Celeste told her.

"How did this happen? Did thee not watch for the creature?"

"I watched, and I instructed her to keep walking," Celeste replied. "But she is stubborn and questions everything."

"Truth. Perchance this lesson doth not snatch life from her. I do have the greatest hope for this child, she may be the one."

"Are you sure?" Celeste asked, sitting next to the woman.

She nodded, adding a handful of herbs to the pot as she stirred. "I am hopeful," she said quietly.

"It has been so long," Celeste whispered.

"Aye, perchance she doth survive she will remember what hast been taught."

Folding her arms around her knees, Celeste gently rocked.

"We have waited so long." She glanced over at the girl. "And now we might lose her to the creature."

"Aye," she whispered, lifting the pot and wafting it under her nose.

She placed the pot on the edge of the fire stones and added more herbs.

"Mother, I am afraid."

"Fear must not settle in thy heart, thou dost know what must be done to rid the body of the poison."

"I know… yet, I am afraid."

"Thy choice be simple, let the fear consume thee, or do what must be done. We are teaching the child to conquer the very thing that consumes thee?"

"No mother I will not be consumed with fear. I speak the words so my feelings may see the truth," she said gently.

"I have the one child to tend to," she said glancing at the girl wrestling with her nightmares. "I cannot tend to another."

"I know," she whispered. Kneeling down, she lifted the hand that wore the red cord and looked closely. "It has burned deeply. The cord is fused with flesh."

The woman sat next to her and looked closely at the charred flesh.

"It be not time to remove the cord," she said, holding Celeste's eyes.

"Only when it be time for the quest can it be cut."

"So, it is to be left?"

"Aye, soothe with the balm of the Aloe plant, thou must leave the cord."

"This has never happened before."

"Nay it hath not, and so we do as has always been done. The cord stays, aye it be fused to the skin, but to remove." She shook her head, leaving the sentence unfinished.

"Is the tincture ready," Celeste asked, swabbing the wrist with Aloe.

"It will be ready when it is ready," the woman said, looking into the fire.

"What do you look for?" Celeste asked.

"Many things, I look for many things," she whispered.

Standing in silence, peering into the flames, she waited.

Placing a wet cloth on the girl's head, Celeste gently stroked her hair. Her body became rigid, her arms struck out. A scream crawled through her finding an escape through clenched teeth.

Turning away from the fire the woman moved to the girl, kneeling down she took her hand, "It begins."

ressing the spoon against her lips, the dark tincture ran down the side of her mouth.

"Drink, thee must to drink," the woman encouraged.

Slapping her hand away, the girl pushed against the mattress.

"Nay, I will not fight thee," she said softly, pushing her gently back on to the mattress.

Mumbling she fought the arms that held her.

"Celeste, come, hold her head, she must drink."

Cradling the child's head in her hands, Celeste groaned silently while the girl fought against her.

"Be still," she whispered.

Tilting the girl's head back, the spoon forced between her lips, she waited for the tincture to move its way down her throat.

"Twill be a long night," the woman said softly, grabbing the girl's hand.

"Leave me," the girl screamed.

"Nay, thee will drink."

"Nay, I will not," she screamed.

Smiling, she picked up the mug of tincture and brought it to the girl's lips. Holding her jaw, she forced the bitter liquid into her mouth. Celeste tilted her head back when the woman placed her hand over the girl's' lips.

"She be stubborn," she said looking at Celeste.

"Aye," Celeste breathed.

"But I more so."

Laying her head gently on the pillow, Celeste moved to the side of the girl and took her hand. Running her eyes over her arm, she looked for signs of the poison. Blue-black lines ran from her fingers to her elbow. Lifting her skirt, she looked for the same on the girl's legs.

"We know it be there, why dost thou look?"

"I had hoped it would not be this bad."

"Truly?...The tincture will calm for the short while. We must gather the things which will be needed,.. Thou knowest thy role in this?"

Celeste nodded.

"Doth fear still taunt thee?"

"Fear no longer stalks," Celeste said softly.

"This be good." She reached for Celeste's hand and squeezed it gently. "Go prepare for what is to come."

Watching Celeste, her head bowed, legs crossed, she pushed up from the ground. Gathering sage into a bundle she tied it with a woven reed. Placing another log on the fire, she worried the coals and watched the smoke curl into the night sky. Laying the sage on the coals, she closed her eyes, breathing in the pungent fragrance.

"Ancients of old who walk unfettered and untamed, I call to thee," she said softly. "Thy counsel be sought, thy wisdom bidden. If it pleases thee, stand before me, that we might speak together."
The fire crackled and spat, the smoke thick and acrid, sparks flew from the coals, she took a small step back and waited.

"Who doth summon the council?" a voice, deep and mystical asked.

"Alathia, Guardian of the keep," she said softly.

"What seekest thou?"

"Thy wisdom."

Smoke curled, draping over her, enveloping her fully.

"Speak."

"Thank thee, the child be filled with the poison of the creature."

"Thou hast the cure for such."

"Aye, this child be not like the others, the cord be fused to the flesh."

"Thou hast removed the cord?"

"Nay."

“What seekest thou?”

“Knowledge, should the cord be cut and rebound?”

“The cutting of the cord be done once the quest begins. To cut now will be death, to leave fused as it be, is uncertain, knowledge of this we do not have.”

“The poison be strong in the child, the cord hath cut deeply, the flesh be charred, the cord and flesh hath become one,” Alathia said.

“Then the weaving be fraught with danger. Thou must do what thy heart instructs.”

The smoke became still and gently wafted into the night sky. Sitting slowly, Alathia rested her head in her hands, the weight of the weaving, heavy.

*F*luttering around Alathia, the dragon settled on her knee and folded his wings.

"My name you called?" he sang.

"Aye, Zoloyth I have need of thee," she said.

"Mistress tell me what you need, and I will do the deed," he sang.

A smile moved slowly across Alathia's face as she looked into the deep red of the dragon's eyes.

"Thy true self I do need of thee," she said softly.

"Oh, this I did not know," he sang.

"Zoloyth, the child be sickened with poison, the dream walk Celeste will do. I need thee to stand guard and thy mystical knowledge we may need."

"All of me you wish to see?"

"Aye," she said softly.

"Never have you asked all of me to see."

"This be truth. The creature has deeply burrowed, the poison doth eat the very marrow of her bones. Zoloyth, this be something that hath not been, I am fearful for her life."

"Mistress," he said quietly.

"Hush." She ran her finger gently over his head. "All of thee. Bridle thy tongue, cease with riddles and the mischief of words. I have need of thee Zoloyth, never have I ask this, I pray never again will it be so. Tarry no longer my friend, do what thou must do, return when thou art truly ready."

Unfolding his wings, he lifted his head, a tiny tear ran down his emerald green cheek and dropped silently on to her lap.

"Oh my friend, do not weep for what is," she said gently.

"I weep for what might be," he replied.

Sighing deeply, she stroked his wing. "Tarry no longer, time be short."

Hovering above her, he circled once and then was gone.

Poking the fire Alathia, stirred the hot coals, lifting the large pot that sat beside her she placed it against the fire stones. Standing slowly she walked with caution toward Celeste.

"Celeste thou art ready?" she asked quietly.

"I am," she breathed.

"We wait for Zoloyth."

Easing down on to the ground, she pulled Celeste into her arms and held her tightly. "We wait like this, aye?"

Resting her head against the purple shawl, Celeste nodded.

The night filled with a loud humming. The breeze grew stronger, shadows danced and caressed the young girl as she fought the poison. The humming became a roar. Green and red filled the night sky, the stars overshadowed by the expanse of wings.

"He is here," Celeste said.

"Aye," Alathia whispered, kissing the top of Celeste's head. "It begins."

Placing his talons gently on the ground, Zoloyth folded his wings and looked down at Alathia. The emerald green of his scales glinted in the fire light, the deep red of his eyes pierced the darkness. He stepped cautiously toward the girl.

"Thou art beautiful," Alathia said, looking up at him.

Eyes dancing with the compliment, he bent his knee, unfolded his wings and bowed before her.

"Tis time." She smiled at Zoloyth. "Come, stand guard over all," she said. "Beautiful, yet thy strength and wisdom be fierce."

Their focus on the young girl, Celeste sat crossed legged at the head of the mattress, and gently rested her hand on the girl's forehead. Wings spread, Zoloyth settled on his haunches.

Carrying the large pot, Alathia sat facing Zoloyth. Her body covered in dark blue lines, each pulsing with life, the girl tossed fitfully on the mattress.

"First, the tincture to calm the body," she whispered, forcing the bitter liquid into the girl's mouth. "When thou art ready Celeste, meld together and walk where thou dost need to walk, I will tend to the body."

Legs crossed, leaning forward, Celeste rested both hands gently on the girl's head.

"The meld may be difficult. If the little one held to self her name, it would not be so," she said, looking up at Alathia.

"Aye, but she hath not chosen. Perchance in the walking of the meld it can be done, let it be so."

Resting her forehead on the girl's, she closed her eyes, breathed deeply and slowly, opening to the thoughts. She pushed deeply, searching for the connection, her mind and body closed to the poison that sort to confuse and destroy.

"Child," she whispered. "Come find me, come find me."

Waves of colour filled her vision, her ears silent to the sounds around her. Searching, she melded deeper, pushing past the resistance and the fear.

The words spoken only in her mind, she continued.

"Child, reach for me, take my hand… I am here, reach for me, let me take you from this place to another. Push through the poison and see me."

"I see you."

"Good, now take my hand."

"No."

"Yes little one, come on, take my hand, we will walk from here to there and back again. See the field, the flowers, breathe deeply their perfume."

"No, I have to stay, it bids me stay."

"Fight the bidding, take my hand, reach out."

"Leave."

"Nay. Fight little one, resist the pull of the creature."

Her mind filled with laughter.

"I am not afraid of you," Celeste whispered.

"You should be," the mind voice crackled.

Lifting her head slowly, Celeste breathed deeply and looked down at the young girl. Her legs now wrapped in strips of cloth soaked in herbs, her arms pulsing with blue lines, her eyes closed, she lay still before her.

"Celeste?" Alathia questioned.

She shook her head. "She fights… the poison is strong, it has taken her mind and her words."

The silence of the night was shattered with the deep resonance of his roar. The young girl moved restlessly against the sound. Unfolding his wings, he pushed up from the ground and hovered over them.

"Be at peace Zoloyth," Alathia said, looking up at him. "Celeste, continue with the meld walk."

Gently cradling the young girl's head, Celeste rested her forehead against hers. Searching for a connection she pushed deeply, her hands shaking with the effort.

"Child, don't hide from me," she whispered.

"Help me."

Melding together, Celeste answered with her thoughts.

"Trust me."

Their thoughts became entwined, their vision the same.

"I see you," the child said quietly.

"Take my hand."

Placing her hand in Celeste's, she melded with her. Walking in the melding together, she looked to Celeste.

"What is happening?"

"We walk until it is time to stop, then we return."

"Oh, I feel nothing."

"Aye, choose the place thee would like to walk."

"The place we first met. I want to see the other tapestries."

Celeste smiled. "It is not the time for such. Where else would you like to go?"

"The rooms behind the tapestries."

"Also not the time to do so."

"What is it time for?"

"Walking."

*T*earing strips of cloth, Alathia watched Celeste closely. "It be done," she said, looking up at Zoloyth. "They be melded."

"Mistress the body burns with fever."

"Aye, and it struggles for breath, we must work fast."

"I am ready," he whispered.

"Then it be time," she said quietly.

Taking the girl's arm, she straightened it, one hand under the elbow, the other the wrist. Zoloyth gazed at the cord fused with her flesh, the poison wrapped tightly around the wound.

Lifting a talon, he pierced the vein. The stench of death filled the air. Using his wings for balance, he pushed deeply. The green black of the talon changed to a deep blue as the poison moved slowly into him.

Throwing back his head, he roared deeply, tongues of flames shot from his nostrils. He hovered above her, the talon deeply imbedded in her arm.

Head bowed, Alathia began to chant,

> *"Oh the sting of sorrow pains*
> *Naught but life is to gain;*
> *Deeply does the river flow*
> *Death shall not this child to know;*
> *In the melding peace be sought*
> *Let not this be for naught;*
> *Ancient ones I call to thee*
> *Bind thy wisdom be the plea;*
> *Strength and prudence we take in hand*
> *Together as one we stand;*
> *Naught but life is to gain*
> *Soothe the sting of sorrows pain."*

Firelight cut through the swirling mist casting shadows over the small keep.

Easing the talon from the vein, Zoloyth hovered over the three, the expanse of his wings shielding them. Blue-black fingers curled and twisted from the open wound, snaking toward Celeste.

The stillness was shattered by Zoloyth's roar, flames shot from his nostrils. The fire, seeking its prey, swirled and consumed the blue fingers. Flames leaped and chased searing all it touched.

A fine ash fell gently.

Lowering her arm, Alathia pressed a strip of cloth onto the wound. Flying over to the fire Zoloyth picked up a hot coal. Holding it in his talons he hovered over Alathia. Lifting the cloth, she nodded to him. He placed the hot coal onto the open wound. The smell of searing flesh filled her nostrils as the wound was seared closed, the bleeding stopped. Scooping herbs from the pot, she placed them gently on the seared flesh and bound it firmly.

*M*elded together in thought and vision, she floated in the cool water of the cave. Above her, tiny lights glowed in the darkness. The only sound was the gentle movements she made in the water, the ripples echoing through the cave.

"You have some imagination child," Celeste called from the rock she was sitting on.

"It's nice here," she said softly, kicking her feet gently and floating toward her. "The glow worms are like stars."

"Yes they are," Celeste agreed, looking above her. "What made you think of a place like this?"

"I don't know, it just seemed right to be here." She pulled up on the rock next to Celeste. Scooping a hand full of water she flicked it at her before diving into the clear blue water.

Laughing, Celeste watched her swim without effort, then stop, and float on her back.

"We will be returning soon," she said. "Once the meld is broken, you will feel many things."

"What if I don't want to return?"

"There is no question of want, you need to, therefore you will," Celeste replied.

"What was it that bit me?" she asked, rolling over in the water and swimming toward Celeste.

"The creature, and it did not bite you," she said, as the young girl pulled up on the rock and sat next to her.

"Well what did it do?"

"It moved through you, if you had not moved it would have continued its journey. It settles only when there is movement, and feeds off the one it settles in."

The girl shuddered.

"So it is feeding on me?" she asked with amazement.

"Yes," she whispered. "That is why you are here and not there."

"How did you do this?"

"We did this. We melded our thoughts, creating something that was not, leaving our bodies as they were."

"I don't feel this creature thing," she whispered.

"When we return from the melding, you will feel, you will know," she said softly.

"I don't want to return then," she said defiantly.

"Child, you have no choice. Once the meld is broken, this will be no more. So we can walk back together, or I walk alone, either way this will be no more."

"So I'm not back there?"

"You are, and, you are not."

"I don't understand."

"I know." Celeste rested her hand on her shoulder. "Don't let it trouble you, it will become clear when it is time."

"So many things are unclear."

"I know," she squeezed her shoulder gently, "this too will change."

eleste stretched to ease the tension in her back. Looking around the small shelter, the roaring fire and then down at the young girl, now covered with furs, she sighed.

"What troubles thee?" Alathia asked gently. "Thou art weary from the melding?"

"Some what, Why is the child in a shelter and not within a chamber in the castle?" she asked looking up at the wooden beams above her head.

"We be where we need to be. Rest for the while, then we shall eat." Standing, she rested her hand on a wooden beam.

"What troubles thee?" Alathia asked again.

"The girl needs comfort, rest to fight the poison that remains. And we are in the keep with all the dangers that it brings."

Breathing deeply, Alathia sat on the small stool in front of the fire. Picking up a stick, she prodded the fire gently and then moved hot coals to the side of the fire stones.

"She doth have comfort," she said quietly. "How will a bedchamber with silks and fine linens give to her the healing she doth need?"

"The chambers would be a safer place, and give what is needed," she said, sitting next to Alathia. "Why thinkest thou this?"

"Cast thy eyes upon the keep, now thy mind to the chambers…"

"Oh child," Alathia said gently, touching Celeste on the cheek with her open hand. "Thou feels much for this one?"

"Yes," she whispered.

"On the quest there will not always to be the fine linens and the silks. There will be dangers, and times of deep sorrow. To find what is needed for the body and mind in what thou has, be a lesson well learnt," she said. "Healing will still be, wrapped in furs or in silk, healing be healing."

"This truth I know," Celeste breathed.

"We prepare her for what be ahead, to give knowledge and understanding. Perchance she will recall what hath been taught, this we hope for. We canst allow feelings to shadow what must be done."

"This I also know. My heart is heavy with sorrow… each breath the child takes is filled with pain," she said quietly, looking over at the girl. "Why must it be so?"

"Thou questions the wisdom of the Ancients, what is and always has been?"

"I question the need for the challenges, for the pain and the torment. She is a child."

"Aye, and she hath chosen the quest. That choice doth bring with it the challenges. Do not speak of these things again, thou cannot question what is. She be in the betwixt, as all have been, the choice be hers alone. Perchance she is the one, each challenge prepares for the quest."

Celeste glanced over at the young girl. "We do what is expected, we teach, we speak of those things needful for the quest. When the quest begins, they are lost, shadowed by the very nature of the quest itself… There be times I question all that is done." Pushing up from the ground she walked to the shelter and took the girl's hand in hers.

"It is what it is," Alathia said, sitting next to her. "To question the wisdom of the Ancients be unwise. It hath always been this way, it will always to be."

"I do not challenge the wisdom of the Ancients, nor do I challenge thee. What is, is, and always will be. I do what I am called to do. I will take the child where she must go, and prepare her for what is ahead."

"I know thy heart," Alathia said gently.

"Thank thee," she said quietly, lifting the cloth on the girl's arm. "The lines are fading, the poison is weak."

"Aye, Zoloyth weaved what must be done, she doth need rest and then the challenges can begin again."

he sky darkened, the air throbbed with the rhythmic sound of Zoloyth's wings. Circling the keep, he threw back his head and roared deeply, cutting through the stillness of the night.

Alathia stood slowly, waiting and watching.

"What is happening?" Celeste asked.

"This I do not know," Alathia said quietly.

Emerald green wings fully expanded, talons clenched, his red eyes piercing the night, he glided to the ground.

"Zoloyth?"

"Mistress, for the girl I have come."

"Why?" Celeste whispered, glancing over at her.

"It is as I say, this be the way."

"Zoloyth, what troubles thee?"

"Troubled deeply I am," he sang.

"Lower thy wings, and speak to me of thy thoughts."

Folding his wings, resting on his talons he squatted on the ground.

"Now magnificent one, say to me."

"The girl I will take, to leave, trouble will make."

"Enough, speak clearly without rhyme," Alathia commanded. "The girl be not yours to take."

"Nor thine to keep," he challenged.

Alathia gently stroked his wing and rested her head against the soft scales.

"Speak the truth, hold nothing from me, thy wisdom I will hear."

"Mistress, the creature lurks. It seeks all. I will take the child so all are safe."

"What danger dost thou see?"

Shaking his wing, he moved away from her. "It is best not spoken."

"Show me thy talon."

His roar filled the night like a thunderclap, his eyes ablaze.

"Show me," she insisted. "The poison be still in thee, come my friend thou must rest."

"You challenge me?" he growled.

"Nay, I ask thee to rest and allow the herbs to heal the pain of the creature that twists through thee."

"Care I do not need," he roared, standing to his full height and looking down at her. "All of me to see you did ask, and now I stand before thee, all of me."

"Aye, I did ask this of thee, and now I ask of thee to rest and let the herbs sooth."

"Herbs I do not need. The child I will take."

"I canst let thee take the child, it be not the way."

"It be not thy way. The child I will take. I need not thy consent, thy herbs, or thy consoling words."

He spread his wings, and reached for the mattress with his talon.

"Nay, Zoloyth, I forbid thee."

"Forbid me?....I think not, it will do well for you to remember your place mistress." He turned to her, his eyes piercing the darkness.

"Thou must step back, leave the child as she be."

Throwing back his head, he roared deeply. Flames licked the shelter, seeking to devour the wooden frame.

"Now she must be moved," he said, the flames burning fiercely. Stepping into the chaos, he gathered the edges of the mattress in his talons, spread his wings, and pushed off from the ground.

$\mathcal{F}$rigid wind wrapped around her, each breath burned with the pain of the cold that enveloped her.

Gently lowering the mattress to the ground, Zoloyth stepped back, his eyes fixed on the entrance to the cave.

"Phiobe," he roared.

Furs covering the cave entrance parted. A tall man, his face weathered by the elements, looked over at Zoloyth. Hair, black as the darkest night, long and untamed, danced in the wind.

"Master?"

"Into the cave the girl you will take. Warmth and comfort you will make."

"Why have you done this?"

"Phiobe, do not question me," he roared. "If she is the one, then she needs to be here."

"If she is not the one?" he asked, bending his knees and sliding his hands under the sleeping figure.

"Then this will be for naught," Zoloyth sang.

"What sayeth Alathia of thy plan?"

"The plan she doth not to know…. Take the child into the warmth of the cave, wrap her well in the furs and stoke the fire."

Standing slowly, he lifted the girl and held her tightly.

"And thee?" Phiobe asked carefully.

Tilting his head to the side, Zoloyth looked down at the child. His gaze, tender and filled with concern, he spread his wing. "Safety I will ensure."

"So be it," Phiobe whispered, cradling the child to him.

Gently brushing the swirling snowflakes from her face, he stamped his feet before entering the cave. Restless and cold, she pushed against him. Eyes closed, lost in exhaustion and the dreams that filled her mind, she fought the cold and the feelings that consumed her.

"Hush child," he whispered, laying her gently on the raised bed.

Draping the furs over her, he looked down at the innocent face.

"If only," he whispered, turning toward the hearth that sat in the middle of the cave. Adding more wood to the fire, he moved to the hewn shelves. Running his fingers over the purple bottles he looked for the tincture that would ease the pain of the poison.

"Celeste?" the innocent voice whispered through the cave.

Moving quickly, he sat beside her, running his callused hand over her forehead.

"Shh, rest child," he whispered.

Her eyes fluttered open, resting on the unfamiliar face. Fear ran through her, weighting her with uncertainty.

"Ohhh," she breathed.

"You are safe, be still child and rest," he said gently.

"So cold," she said, trying to control the shivers that assaulted her.

Draping another fur over her, he moved quickly to the fire and added more wood.

"Better?" he asked.

Nodding, she pulled the soft fur to her chin and peered at him, her eyes filled with uncertainty.

"You are with Zoloyth, this is his lair. You need to rest child."

"Who?" she asked, through chattering teeth.

"Rest," he whispered, stroking her hair gently.

Her face wet with tears, her body aching from the cold and the pain of the poison, she held his hand tightly.

Lifting the mug from the floor he held it to her lips.

"Drink little one, it is warm and will help you sleep."

Sipping the warm liquid she held his eyes, while he softly sang:

> *"Sleep oh sleep my precious child*
> *Rest thy weary eyes;*
> *The sun's head rests on the mountain rise*
> *Rest thy weary eyes;*
> *Angel child, thy dreams be sweet*
> *On the morrow again we meet;*
> *Sleep oh sleep my precious child*
> *Close thy weary eyes."*

Gently lowering her head, he stroked her hair while he sang. Closing her eyes, she drifted into a restless sleep.

*H*ead down, nuzzling against Celeste, the white stallion stood patiently.

"What thinkest thou?" Alathia asked.

"To bring the child to the place she needs to be," she said, running her hand over the long mane.

"I forbid thee," her hand resting on the snout, she held Celeste's eyes, "thee will wait."

"Nay, three days of fast riding and I will be at Zoloyths lair."

"Say to me how thee will ascend the mountain, the climb alone be three or four days."

"I will ask the winged ones to take me."

"Nay, it be certain death for the one who carries thee, I forbid thee."

She slapped the stallion gently on the rump. "Enough Celeste, thee waits." Arms folded, she nodded to the stallion. Raising his head, he nuzzled her gently before cantering away.

"Tis time for thee to put aside the notion of retrieving the child. Tis time to trust Zoloyth, he will not permit harm to befall her."

"Hollow words mother. Thee sees fit to say these things to me, after thy own challenge of Zoloyth's actions?" Celeste asked with defiance.

"Aye," she whispered, unfolding her arms she moved closer to Celeste. "It is what it is, we have much work to do for when the child returns. So, thee can stand with thy face set in anger, or do what is needful."

"It doth not feel right," she whispered.

"Not right or wrong, it be different," Alathia said gently.

Taking Celeste's hand she led her toward the fire.

"Thou must eat. Sit, let me serve thee," Alathia said, kneeling down in front of the fire.

Brushing the coals to one side and sliding a stick under the burnt leaves, she lifted them gently and laid them on the edge of the fire stones.

"Fish?" Celeste asked.

"Aye, fish."

Opening the leaves carefully, shaking her fingers against the steam that curled and singed, Alathia opened each bundle. Sprinkling herbs over the fish, she stood slowly, and moved her stool closer to the fire.

"I canst eat for thee." She looked over at Celeste and smiled. "That, thee must do for self."

"Really?" she whispered.

"Aye, now move thy stool closer, and eat, then we will secure the keep and rest."

*T*owering over the bed, Zoloyth peered down at the young girl. Reaching out with his wing he touched her face gently, his eyes wet with unshed tears. Settling on his haunches, he turned to Phiobe.

"She sleeps?"

"Aye," he said quietly.

"She has had tincture for the poison?"

"Aye."

"Has she eaten?" Zoloyth asked

Shaking his head, he moved closer to the bed, sat down next to Zoloyth and crossed his legs.

"She must eat."

"This I know," he replied quietly.

Snuggled into the furs, the child listened to the exchange of words. Opening her eyes slightly, she peered at the dragon through her dark lashes.

Phiobe nudged Zoloyth with his shoulder, and tilted his head toward the girl.

"So, you are not asleep little one?" Phiobe asked gently.

"No," she whispered, opening her eyes and smiling at him.

"This is Zoloyth."

Sitting up and pulling the fur to her, she rested her chin on her knees. Eyes filled with wonder she stared at the dragon before her.

"Be not afraid little one," Zoloyth said gently. "We have met before, do you remember?"

Lifting her chin and unwrapping her hand from the fur, she moved her thumb toward her fingers and smiled.

"Yes, I was that size," he whispered.

In awe of his magnificence she reached out to touch him. He moved closer. She ran her fingers gently over his emerald green scales, and looked into eyes filled with tenderness.

"Beautiful," she whispered. "But so big."

"Yes little one," Phiobe said. "Now drink this." He handed her a steaming mug. "It is broth it will warm and strengthen."

Taking the mug, she peered through the steam at him before tentatively sipping from the ceramic edge. "It's nice," the girl whispered.

"Good, drink all of it," Zoloyth told her. "Then you and I are going to fly together."

"Really?"

"Yes little one, but first, you must drink the broth."

"Master?" Phiobe turned to him, his eyes filled with questions.

"It will be as I said," Zoloyth told him, rising from the cave floor and standing to his full height.

"The lessons begin tonight."

Stars, bright and beautiful filled her eyes with a delight she had not known. Green and pink aurorae swirled and danced, the colours crisp and clear, their beauty adding mystical notes to the peaks of the mountains.

White streaks of lightening cut through the colours before her, the sky pulsed with life and expectation.

Moving freely, without fear, saturated with the beauty around her, it was some time before she realised that the warm talons no longer held her.

The rhythmic sounds of his wings distant, the cold piercing, falling freely through the thin air, she looked up at him.

Tongues of fear moved quickly, sucking the cold air deeply into her lungs, she waited. Closing her eyes, she fought the fear, untying it from the fringes of her mind and shaking it free.

Zoloyth swooped, the air pulsed with the speed of his descent. Hovering, he waited, catching her and holding her tightly to him.

Laughing, she stroked him gently and snuggled against him. His wings cutting through the frigid air he hovered over the lair before placing her gently on the fallen snow.

Running toward the covering of the cave, she squeezed between the furs and ran to the fire. Rubbing her hands together and stamping her feet, she breathed in the warmth.

“Little one, your lips are blue with cold,” Phiobe said, concern and anger tempering the words.

Unable to control the chattering of her teeth, she nodded.

Wrapping her in a fur he rubbed her arms briskly, muttering to himself as he did so.

Cold pierced the lair when Zoloyth pulled aside the furs and strode to the fire.

"She is freezing, what did you do?" Phiobe asked.

His eyes twinkling, a smile settling on the corners of his mouth, Zoloyth settled near the fire.

"We flew."

Giggling, she ran to Zoloyth, nestling against him, the fur wrapped tightly around her.

Moving to a shelf that had been hewn from the rock, Phiobe picked up a bundle of white furs, and then sat down next to the girl.

"Give me your foot," he said gently.

Leaning against Zoloyth, she rested her leg on his.

"This will keep your feet and legs warm," he said. Laying the fur against her leg, he fashioned a covering for her foot. Piercing the hide with a long needle threaded with leather thong, he began to lace the fur.

"It tickles," she said softly.

Running her hand over the hide, she smiled at him and placed her other leg on his.

"So, little one," Zoloyth said quietly. "Were you afraid when you realised I was not holding you?"

Leaning back and looking up at him, she shook her head.

"Nay?" he questioned.

"I knew you would catch me," she said with confidence.

"And this you knew, how?"

"Why wouldn't you?" she challenged. "Besides what would you tell Celeste?"

Laughing he shook his head. "Fear thee did not know?" he asked again.

Lifting her hand she moved her thumb towards her fingers. "Maybe this much," she said.

"Trust is not an easy thing little one. Why did you trust me to catch you?"

Watching the needle as it pierced the hide, she took time with her answer.

"I was a little afraid," she whispered, looking up at him. "But it was so beautiful the colours dancing on the mountain, the stars watching us. Then I realised you weren't there."

"And?" he encouraged her.

"And, I thought you will be there when the time is right, and you were," she said resting her head against him.

"Aye," he whispered looking over at Phiobe.

Smiling, Phiobe tied the ends of the laces and patted the girls' leg. "All done little one," he said, moving her leg gently from his and standing slowly. "She is asleep I think." Kneeling down, and sliding his arms under her he lifted her gently, and laid her on the bed.

"She sleeps this time?" Zoloyth asked.

"Aye," he replied, covering her with the furs and touching her cheek, "she sleeps."

ent over the bench Phiobe worked silently. Scales fell quickly under the knife, his mind filled with thoughts of the child. Looking down in response to the tug on his sleeve, he looked into her dark eyes and smiled.

"So you are awake little one," he said softly.

"Yes, where is Zoloyth?"

"He is not here."

"Where is he?"

"If he had wanted you to know, he would have awoken you and told you," he said, turning back to scaling the fish.

Troubled by her silence he lay down the knife, turned and knelt down, taking her hands in his.

"Little one, what troubles you?"

Looking at the binding on her wrist, a tear travelled silently down her cheek.

"Ahh, you are in pain little one?"

Nodding, she looked into his eyes.

Lifting her from the cave floor, he held her tightly.

"Let me tend to your arm," he sat her on the bench, "then we will eat."

"The woman used some herbs," she said quietly.

"Yes, her name is Alathia," he smiled, "she is a healer, as am I." Removing the cloth, he looked closely at her wrist.

"Phiobe, where is the red cord?"

"It is still there."

"But I don't see it, how can it be long enough to reach here?"

Gently dabbing the scarred wrist, he looked up at her.

"Because you cannot see it, does it mean it is not?" Pursing her lips she tilted her head, deep in thought.

"No," she whispered.

"Then it is still as it was," he smiled, "now this might sting," he said, gently dabbing a lotion on the seared flesh.

"Phiobe, what is a healer?"

"It is one who heals," he said quietly.

"Heals what?"

"That which needs healing."

"Am I a healer?"

"On your quest you may be asked to be so," he said, trying to hide his surprise at her question.

"Can all things be healed if healing is needed," she asked carefully. Placing the bottle of tincture on the bench, he rested his hand on her head and looked deeply into her eyes.

"No, not all things can be healed."

"Then what good is a healer if not all things can be healed?" she challenged.

Smiling he looked away, ordering his thoughts.

"See the fish," he pointed towards them, "they are beyond healing."

Tilting her head to the side she looked at the fish and then at Phiobe.

"So death cannot be healed?"

"No little one."

Breathing out deeply, running her tongue over her lips, deep in thought, she looked back at Phiobe.

"But you caused the fish to die by catching them."

Taken aback with her answer, Phiobe focused on bandaging her wrist.

"The fish chose to take the bait, its death now gives life to another," he said, after some thought.

"So the bear," she ran her hand over the fur boots laced to her legs, "also chose to give his life to keep me warm?"

Rinsing his hands in a bowl of water and wiping them on the cloth next to the bowl, he turned to look at her.

"No," he said quietly, "I chose to take the bear's life."

"But you are a healer," she replied quickly, "how could you do that?"

Shaking his head in disbelief, he touched her gently on the cheek, and held her eyes.

"It was needful, for warmth, for food, for shelter."

"So causing death when it is needful is allowed?" she asked with innocence.

Looking down he ordered his thoughts.

"At times yes," he replied carefully.

"Will I need to cause death?"

"Ahh little one, so many questions," he said, pushing away from her and folding his arms.

"Well, will I?" she asked again.

"Maybe," he said quietly.

"Maybe," she whispered. "Phiobe, how will I know what to do?"

"You will know," he answered quickly.

"Will I know how to heal also?"

Sighing deeply, he moved back to the fish and picked up the knife.

"Yes, you will know, if you remember what has been taught, you will know," he said quietly.

"I don't understand why you think the fish chose death," she said after a few minutes of silence.

"It took the bait. It could have swum past it, but it chose to take the bait, to not see the hook and respond only to its need for hunger."

"Oh," she breathed, deep in thought. "And the bear?"

The knife poised over the fish, he turned to look at her: "I made the choice for him."

"Then the bear should be honoured more," she whispered.

*L*anding softly, Zoloyth held Alathia's eyes, bending a knee he moved his wing in front of him and bowed before her.

"Mistress," he said quietly.

"Zoloyth," she acknowledged. "Where be the child?"

"Safe she is," he sang softly.

"Truth thee speaks?"

"It is as I say," he sang.

Sighing deeply, she sat on the small stool by the fire. Picking up a stick she twirled it in her fingers.

"Why did thee take the child?"

"For safety I did take, trouble I did not make."

"Zoloyth please, I be not a child whom thou must set at ease with rhyme and songs."

"Nay, thee are not," he said quietly.

"Do not mock me," she challenged.

"I do not mock thee, I wrap my words in the cloth of the ancient tongue in respect for thee," he said quietly, sitting slowly and settling.

"The child be taken for her safety, she has much to learn, and of this I will teach."

"It be not thy role to teach, this be given to others."

"So thee says," he challenged.

"So the Ancients say."

Shrugging, he leaned forward.

"The creature lurks, from this I protect," he said.

"This I know."

"Yet thee stays in the keep. Where be thy guards, where be thy protectors?" he challenged.

"I have no need. I do know the enemy well."

"Knowledge doth not protect from its sting."

"Nay it doth not. To know thy enemy be one thing. To know where he doth lurk gives advantage in battle," she said quietly.

"Aye that is truth. Can thee win this battle?"

"I do not battle with that which be less powerful than I."

"Interesting stand thou dost take," he challenged.

"Thee knows my power Zoloyth, greater than thee in some ways I am."

"Truth, yet thy shelter be broken and charred, thou hast not repaired. With thy power one would to think this be done."

"I will not ask of another tree to lay down its life to shelter me," she snapped. "It is what it is, and so it shall remain as such."

"Yet, thee can command and it will be done, or thee can summon others to do for thee," he replied.

"Why summon another when I can do? My back be strong, my hands, nimble."

"Aye," he smiled, "yet thou still dost not have shelter."

"So thee says, yet it is because of thy actions I do not."

"Aye," he chuckled. "Then I should repair for thee."

Poking the fire with the stick, watching the sparks and the curling of the smoke, she waited.

"Mistress, the child be the one," he whispered.

"Aye," lifting her head slowly, she looked into his eyes, "this truth I do know."

*L*ying in the fields of flowers, staring up at the morning sky, Celeste stilled her thoughts and reached for the child. Her breathing controlled, her focus sharp and attuned to the beating of her heart, she walked the meld.

"Child, hear me," she whispered. "I am here."

Waiting, her body still, her mind open to the meld, she searched.

"Child, it is Celeste, be not afraid of what you hear, reach for me."

"Celeste?" a whispered innocence filled her mind.

"Yes, I am here."

Her eyes closed, still sitting on the bench, she swung her legs in rhythm to the beat of her heart.

"Are you safe?"

"Yes, Phiobe is here."

"Good, I miss you," Celeste whispered, a tear moving freely down her cheek.

"I am learning."

"What do you learn?"

"Of healing and of death."

"Difficult lessons little one."

"No, it is what it is," she whispered.

"Can you see me?" Celeste asked.

"Yes, you are in the field."

Sighing deeply, connected completely with the child, she searched for the poison.

"Yes, and you are in Zoloyths lair."

"I am."

The vision of her smile filled Celeste's mind.

"I like Zoloyth," the child whispered.

"Good, how do you feel?"

"Cold." She laughed.

"Yes, the snow falls deeply on the mountains."

"Celeste, I do not want to be a healer," she whispered, reaching for her hand.

"Why, little one?"

Lying down in the field next to Celeste she rested her head on her shoulder.

"Why be a healer if all cannot be healed?"

"A healer heals only those things that can be," she said gently, "of the other things it will be as it is written to be."

"Still, I don't think I want to be one."

"Sometimes we do not have a choice. We do what must be done at the time it is asked of us or we see the need," Celeste replied carefully.

"What if I don't see the need?"

"With your eyes maybe you won't see, but with your heart you will see so much more than your eyes ever will."

"Like how I see you now?"

"Yes," she whispered, stroking the head that rested on her shoulder.

"I feel you stroking my head," she smiled, "can you feel me?"

"Yes little one."

"Celeste, I don't want to be a fish," she whispered, lifting her head from her shoulder and looking into her eyes.

"What do you mean?" Celeste asked, puzzled by the comment.

"To be so hungry that I don't see the hook."

*H*ands resting on the bench, Phiobe stared at her face. Her eyes closed, a smile settled comfortably on her lips, relaxed and at ease, she sat on the bench, her body held in stillness.

"Little one," he whispered again.

"I have to go," she whispered to Celeste, "he calls me."

"Go," reaching up she cupped her face with her hands and gently kissed her cheek, "remember you can always reach for me."

Opening her eyes slowly, she looked into Phiobe's and smiled.

"Where have you been?" he asked gently.

"In the field with Celeste."

"Oh, so you can meld?"

"Yes." She laughed. "Can't you?"

"No," he smiled, "come the fish is ready, we must eat," he lifted her from the bench and set her down gently. "Zoloyth will return soon, we need to be ready."

"Ready for what?" she asked, sitting on the stool next to the fire.

"Ready for his return, for the journey you will make today," he said, handing her a plate of fish, "now, eat."

Lifting a piece of fish with her fingers she brought it slowly to her mouth, her hand poised, she looked up at Phiobe.

"What is wrong?"

"We need to honour the fish," she whispered, "thank it for its stupidity."

Suppressing a smile, he moved a stool next to her, resting his plate of fish on his knees.

"How would you like to do that?" he asked, the smile held captive by an act of will.

She looked at him carefully, "I don't know," she smiled, "maybe he would be insulted to be reminded of his stupidity."

Laughing, he looked down at his plate. "Maybe so, but we thank him anyway," he said, breaking a piece and popping it into his mouth. Chewing slowly, his eyes twinkling, he turned to look at her.

"You know something little one," he swallowed, and continued, "you are truly one of a kind."

"Is that good?"

"Oh yes," wiping his hand over his mouth, "it is little one, it is."

The corners of the fur clasped tightly in his talons, Zoloyth glanced down at his cargo before hovering above his lair.

Snuggled into the fur, the young girl rested her head on Phiobe, closing her eyes she listened to the sound of Zoloyth's wings and the whistling of the cold wind as they flew.

"Where are we going?" she asked, opening her eyes and looking up at Phiobe.

"To the castle," lowering his head to hear her better, "and there are some things you need to know."

"What things?"

"You must do exactly as you are told," he held her eyes, watching for any flicker of rebellion. "You must not leave my side, you must not wander away from either Celeste or I."

"Celeste will be there?"

"Yes, Zoloyth will be waiting for us outside the castle."

"Why are we going to the castle?"

"It is time that is why. Remember what I have told you. No matter what you see or hear, you must not leave my side."

"Why?"

"It is the way it must be done."

"Phiobe," she looked up at him, "why is that always the answer, always?"

Smiling, he held her eyes, "because it is the truth," he said gently.

Zoloyth rested the fur on the ground, unclasped his talons and landed next to them.

"We are here," he sang.

Uncurling her legs she stood slowly, shielding her eyes from the sun that warmed her.

"We are here," she whispered.

"Yes little one," Phiobe said, taking her hand in his, "come we must find Celeste, and then we can enter the castle."

Walking slowly together, the castle looming before her, she studied it closely.

Shimmering in the morning sun, turrets reached toward the clouds. Each stone appeared to breathe in the land around it. Changing colours of greens and brown, melted into the soft yellow cream of sandstone.

The drawbridge had been lowered and the entrance was dark and unwelcoming. Squeezing his hand tighter, she slowed her pace, wrestling the uncertainty that wrapped tightly around her mind.

"Celeste waits," he said, "come child."

Reaching for Celeste, melding to her thoughts, she felt for the emotions she may hold. A sense of peace and calmness caressed her mind, gently lifting the fingers of uncertainty.

"Peace child," her mind and body echoed with the gentleness of her voice, "walk quickly, I wait for you."

"Child," Phiobe said, "are you alright?"

"Yes," she smiled.

*E*yes closed, Alathia tamed her thoughts, her focus on Celeste. Melding with her, she searched for knowledge of the child. The sound of Zoloyth settling on the ground broke the meld. Opening her eyes she looked over at him.

"Zoloyth, I did not expect to see thee," she said quietly.

"You wish I should go?"

"Nay," she smiled, "tell me of the child and all that has happened."

Standing slowly, she moved her stool against the upright pillar of the small shelter. Sitting, she stretched her legs and leaned against it, resting her hands in her lap.

"Tired you are?" he sang.

"Nay, worried for the child, for Celeste. I do not think this challenge be necessary," she said quietly.

"Questions you have?"

"Some. What be thy reasoning for the challenge?" Alathia asked.

Bending his knees, he squatted next to her. Folding his wings, and looking down at her, he tilted his head to the side.
"A warrior must to be prepared for all things," he said gently.

"This be truth my friend. Must a warrior be tested beyond the skills he doth have?"

"How else will he learn of his weakness, and hone that weakness to strength?"

"Aye," she sighed. "Thou thinkest the child be such?"

"Dost thee?"

Smiling, she looked up at him and crossed her ankles.

"So we play with words," she challenged.

"Nay mistress, I ask only what thou believes of a warrior," he replied, his eyes twinkling with mischief.

"The warrior must be prepared, to know the enemy more so than the enemy knows self. He must to see further than the blood lust or the need to defend. To know when to lay the weapon down, be wisdom. At times, strategy be a greater weapon than force."

"Be it not wise to prepare one for such?"

"Aye, it be wisdom. Still the challenge I do question," she replied.

"What be thy reasoning?"

"Ahh Zoloyth, we speak of a child, one who be steeped in innocence. Whose heart hath not known deep sorrow, or whose eyes hath not seen despair on another's face."

"Truth. To hone the strength needed, the challenge be set. She is well protected, Phiobe be with them."

"Aye," she breathed. "Yet my heart be heavy with worry."

"Then this be thy challenge," he replied gently, "the challenge of letting go, of trusting those who be with her. Of putting aside thy fear and allowing the child to be equipped."

"Wise words my friend," she said quietly.

haking her hand free, she ran to Celeste. Kneeling down, her arms open, Celeste smiled when she fell into her.

"Little one," Celeste whispered.

Burying her face into Celeste's shoulder, the child held her tightly.

"Celeste," her voice broke with emotion.

Glancing up at Phiobe, Celeste acknowledged his presence. Easing back the cloak he wore, he ran his fingers over the dagger strapped to his side.

Gently easing away from the child, she stood.

Lifting her skirt she showed him the dagger strapped to her leg. Dropping her skirt quickly she took the child's hand in hers.

"Where are we going?" the child asked with innocence.

"You will see soon enough," Phiobe told her. Kneeling down, he took both her hands in his. "Now, you must stay with us, do not wander away, do not be enticed to explore on your own."

She nodded, staring into his eyes.

"Why?" she whispered.

"You do not need a reason," he said.

"Now, come little one," Celeste said gently, holding out her hand, "we have much to do."

Walking between them she peered into the darkness of the castle. Their steps echoed on the sandstone, her eyes filled with wonder.

"We are here," Celeste said, stopping in front of the large wooden door.

Leaning back, the child looked up at the huge tapestry hanging over the door. Filled with expectation, she waited for it to begin its dance.

"Come on," the child whispered.

"Little one?"

"When will it dance like the first one?"

"Tell me what you see," Celeste said gently.

"It's dark, so it's hard to see," she replied.

"Yes it is so. Think back on what you have been shown these past days, look at the tapestry and tell me what you see."

"I see shadows and shapes, the colours are dark," she whispered, reaching for Celeste's hand.

"And?"

"And I don't like it," she said quietly.

"Why?"

"It makes me feel sad," she whispered.

"Move closer," Celeste encouraged.

Shaking her head, she took a step back.

Phiobe lifted her gently from the floor. "Now little one, we will move closer together, and then you tell Celeste what you see." "Ready?" Celeste whispered.

He nodded.

The tapestry began to move, gently at first as though pushing away from the door. The child watched, her eyes filled with wonder, her mind bathed in uncertainty. The edges of the tapestry began to curl, moving closer to them. She pulled away, pressing her face into Phiobe's shoulder.

A hot wind danced around them, touching and teasing, stroking Phiobe's cloak. It caressed the child's hair, playing with each strand, and warming the coldness and damp of the castle. Gathering strength it reached for Celeste, swirling around her red dress, tugging at the hem of her skirt.

"Stop," she whispered.

"Peace little one," Celeste said, "open your eyes and tell me what you see."

Lifting her head slowly, she looked first at Celeste and then at the tapestry.

"I see sadness," she whispered, "I feel pain here," she touched her head with the tip of her finger. "The wind burns, it whispers, I don't like what it is saying."

Swirling, the wind became stronger, reaching for all. The tapestry swung out, the edges curling. Stronger the wind swirled, pushing them forward, their clothes dancing and reaching for the tapestry.

Fascination and fear crawled through her, she held tightly to Phiobe. The tapestry extended its reach, pulling them into the darkness. The wind strong and fierce crackled and teased, wrapping the darkness around them.

Voices loud and intrusive broke through the swirling wind. Pressing her face into Phiobe she tried to hide, quelling the fear that settled heavily. Jostled by the crowds pushing past, she clung to him. Lifting her head, she glanced quickly around.

Gentle rain clawed, capturing the smell of damp and rotting foliage, wrapping it tightly around her. The street was crowded with people, rushing and pushing, horses stood restlessly. Dogs wandered freely, untethered and uncontrolled.

"Where are we?" she whispered.

Running her hand gently over her head, Celeste held her eyes.

"Where we need to be," she said, her words captured by the chaos and lost in the noise.

Lowering her to the ground, Phiobe stepped back and took her hand, Celeste moved to the side and grasped her other hand.

"We walk like this," he said, his free hand resting on the hilt of the dagger.

In awe of the sights and sounds, she walked without question.

Children played in the street, taking no thought of the chaos that filled the morning. Mud clung tightly to feet and clothes, dogs snapped at their heels, people yelled and screamed, pushing and shoving, filled with urgency, void of purpose.

"Celeste," she said, looking up at her, "I don't like it here."

"I know child," she said gently, "keep walking."

"No," she yelled, stopping suddenly and shaking her hands free.

"Don't," Celeste said, "fight what you feel, tame it and keep walking."

"No." Stepping around Celeste, she ran towards a group of children.

Shaking her head, Celeste looked to Phiobe, his hand resting on the dagger, he moved quickly toward the group.

Stopped by a hand holding her elbow firmly, Celeste turned. Pulling her arm free, she took a step back.

"Mistress, so very kind of you to join us." The voice deep and sinister escaped from a mouth holding contempt.

"Step back," she said firmly.

Shrugging and tilting his head, he smiled in feign defeat.

"As you say Mistress."

"Silias I will not do battle with you today," she said, her eyes challenging him.

"What a shame," he whispered, moving closer to her. "She will stay, you know this don't you?"

"So you say," she replied, glancing quickly at the group of children.

"I do," the words dripped with sarcasm, "you lose so many here, not that I am ungrateful."

"Step back," she said firmly.

Raising his hands, he took a step back. "Look around you, all these are your doing," he taunted, "each one you have brought here, you have been unable to tame."

Breathing deeply, she held his eyes. "I did not make the choice," she said quietly.

"No," he laughed, "but still you bring them, knowing you will lose them. Knowing that this place fills them with despair, feeds the rebellion, taunts the perception of truth, and gives them a freedom you cannot give."

"So you say," she stepped toward him, anger clawing at her words. "And yet I am here…so we shall see."

"Ahh a challenge is it?"

"No," she glared at him.

Running his finger down her arm, he leaned closer to her.
"She will stay," he whispered.

Stepping back, repulsed by his closeness, she brushed her arm.

"There is much talk of this child," he told her.

Raising her eyebrow, she folded her arms and waited.

"They say she could be the one."

Celeste shrugged, her eyes holding his.

"So what do you say?" he questioned.

"It is what it is," she said firmly.

Laughing, he shook his head. Reaching into his robe, he pulled out a small pouch. "This is the crystal you have tried to take from me for so long, I will exchange it for the child."

"No."

"You know its power Celeste, you know what it can do…what you could do, the power you would have over the Council."

The corner of her mouth moved slightly, her lips tightening. Unfolding her arms, she glared at him.

"I am not called by your thoughts, nor do I have thoughts of power."

"Oh I think you do," opening the pouch he tipped the crystal into his hand, "touch it, feel its power," he challenged.

Stepping back, she waited.

"Watch," he whispered.

Closing his eyes, he breathed out slowly. The crystal hovered above the palm of his hand, pulsing, and radiating light. Buildings began to fade, the street, still and quiet, trees pushed through the ground, twisting and turning, reaching for the sky. The rain ceased, the sky cleared, the sun moved from behind the dark clouds and embraced the trees with warmth.

A hot searing wind swirled around Celeste, colours of green and red danced before her, the group of children and Phiobe faded from her vision.

Raising her arms slowly, palms facing towards Silias, she closed her eyes. White light pulsed from her palms, curling towards the crystal.

The wind became fierce, whipping and tugging at her hair, clawing and pulling, sucking the breath from her.

Still and focused, she stood facing him. The light collided with the red aura. Lightening danced, crackling and fierce, scorching and searing all it touched, it weaved, seeking its prey.

Hovering and twisting, his face masked by the pulsing light of the crystal, he began to shake. Turning on itself, the ground began to move. Small stones flew with force, striking Celeste and falling to be consumed by the dirt they were made from.

Pulling from deep within, she surrounded herself with a blue aura. Reaching for him, trying to meld and capture his thoughts, she pushed deeply.

"You will not win," his voice echoed in her mind.

"Neither will you," she replied, curling her hand and flinging a ball of light.

Consuming the light, the crystal began to hum, resonating with power.

"Thank you," he whispered. Breathing deeply he flung his left hand, red blue light pulsed towards her.

The wind tearing at her gown, lightning striking the ground, wisps of smoke curled from the singed earth. Lifting her arms, fighting against the wind, she pulled in the light from the crystal.

Pain, fierce and burning, seared her mind and body. Her arms shaking, she pushed deeper into the meld, seeking to capture his thoughts and make them her own.

Charged with power, surging with pain, she began to levitate. Static electricity pulsed under her, dirt swirled, small chasms opened beneath her. Pushing deeply, she melded with him, seeking out the source of his thoughts.

Darkness descended, blanketing them with a heavy weight, pierced by the auras and the lightening, it sort to settle.

"I am more than you ever will be," his thoughts echoed.

"So you say."

Pushing deeper, the light intense, heat pulsing from her, she wrapped her mind around the crystal. Caressing it with her thoughts, drawing its power, it pulsed brighter. Flames leapt, searing his hand. He stood steadfast, focused, pouring his power into it and drawing from it.

Summoning the winged ones, he commanded them to find the child.

"No," she screamed, slamming light against him.

Laughing he called to them again. A roaring sound filled the air, competing with the roar of the wind. Seeing through his eyes, she gazed at the winged ones. Grey yellow scales glistened, wings spread, moving with ease against the fierce wind, they circled and waited.

"Go," she told them, "do not do this."

"Do as you are bidden," he commanded, "find the child."

"No, you are not his to be commanded," she yelled.

Circling, the four winged ones waited.

"I command you, find the child, or I will strike you with lightening and take life from you."

Excited by his words, filled with destructive power, lightening snaked toward them.

olling and twisting the ground shook the keep. Alathia jumped from her stool and turned quickly toward the distant castle.

"Celeste," she whispered. "We must go," she turned to Zoloyth

"Nay, it is not ours to do."

Moving quickly to the fire she gathered a bundle of sage and threw it onto the coals. Standing in the smoke she closed her eyes.

> *"Vision sharp and clear*
> *Let my ears now to hear;*
> *Mine eyes to see all that be*
> *Show Celeste to me."*

Breathing deeply, she waited. The smoke curled and twisted, wrapping around her, "Show me," she whispered.

Eyes closed, she searched for Celeste. Her vision clouded by darkness and shapes undefined, she pushed deeper, willing the vision to take shape.

"Show me," she commanded.

The smoke thickening, she slowed her breathing, her hands shaking with fear and the effort of searching.

"Ancients of old I summon thee, please to hear my plea," she whispered.

Smoke billowed and swirled, taking shape and form, circling Alathia.

"Who calls the Ancients?"

"It is I Alathia, keeper of the keep, holder of thy truth," she said softly.

"What is thy bidding?"

"I need thy strength and wisdom to pierce the darkness and see into the castle all that be."

"This vision thou hast."

"Aye, but of this I canst see, there be much darkness, I do fear for

Celeste," she whispered.

"Alathia, this be something for the Council, it be naught something to command of the Ancients," a woman's voice, soft yet commanding cut through the smoke.

"Aye," she whispered, "I need thy vision, thy wisdom."

"Summon the Council," the ancient gently told her. "Trust thy heart Alathia, know that Celeste be equipped for all that be asked of her."

"I fear Silias doth hold her captive," she said, emotion raw and untamed smothering the words.

"Then, it is what it is. The Council will decide."

"I beg thee, do not to leave. Give to me what be needed that I may know, that I may see."

"Alathia, peace. Thy heart fears what cannot be seen, filling thee with terrors that may not be so."

"I beg of thee, plead before thee with all that be within me, give to me the vision needed."

"Thou hast all that be needed," she said gently, "equipped with all that thou wilt ever need. Thou knowest the truth, thou hast the wisdom, thine eyes perceive what is and what shall be. Rest in that truth."

"As thou sayest," she said quietly.

Filled with purpose and intent, fuelled by the battle that raged, driven by unseen thoughts, the creature moved silently, seeking out its prey.

Swirling, the smoke gently kissed her cheek and wafted towards the heavens.

*T*hunder claps echoed and bounced around them. Lightning snaked and flashed, seeking to consume. The winged ones rode the wind, held captive by the thoughts, enthralled by the display of power, hypnotised by the pulsing crystal.

"Enough," Celeste yelled, flinging white balls of light at Silias. "Listen to me beautiful creatures, you are free to do as you chose, you are not bound to any commands."

Pushing deeply, Celeste pulled him closer, drawing him with power and thoughts of taking her power.

"Go," she whispered, releasing them from captive thought.

Circling once, they swooped over her. Lowering their beaked heads in salute, they soared through the darkness.

Hovering, Celeste began to circle Silias. Bolts of lightning flew from her fingers, searing the ground around him.

"It is over Silias."

Capturing the wind with her thoughts, she pulled it closer to her, swirling and throbbing with expectation it moved at her will. Moving her hands in a circular motion, she pulled it closer still, threading it with strands of power.

Shaking with the effort of controlling the crystal, his mind awash with thoughts not his own, his body tired and racked with pain, he glanced quickly at the crystal.

"Now," she commanded.

Hot, flamed with power, commanded to obedience, the wind swirled. Wrapping tightly around Silias it squeezed, withholding breath from him, slapping against the shaking hand that held the crystal. Trembling with effort, overcome by the power of the wind, and the thoughts that assailed him, he lowered his hand. Wrapping around the falling crystal, the wind lowered it gently to the ground, then became still.

Pulling the lightning to her, drawing in its power, Celeste moved around him. Tongues of light shot from her feet, burning the scorched earth. Breathing deeply, she closed her eyes, pulled back from the meld and gently lowered her feet to the ground.

Trees were sucked down into the belly of the earth. The scorched soil became a muddy street. Buildings flickered and shimmered, taking shape, becoming solid structures. Rain fell gently, bringing a mist that swirled and caressed with dampness. The squeals of children replaced the silence.

Standing slowly, Silias reached for the crystal. Holding it carefully he placed it into the pouch and tucked it inside his cloak.

Weary, shaking with unspent power Celeste watched him closely.

"Go," she whispered, leaning heavily against the side of the building.

Mud splashing with each rhythmic step, Phiobe ran to her, grabbing her by the arm he pulled her to him.

"Are you alright?" he whispered.

"Yes, where is the child?"

He pulled back, holding her eyes, her flesh hot to the touch and pulsing with power.

"I do not know," he whispered.

*F*alling to her knees, overcome with the vision that had filled her mind, she breathed deeply. Clenching her hands, fighting the emotions, fearful for the child, taking captive each thought, she wrapped it with truth.

"Alathia, do not move," Zoloyth said quietly. "The creature is at the hem of thy garment."

Emptying her mind of all thoughts, relaxing the muscles in her shoulders, letting go the tension held in clenched hands, she waited.

Her feet began to tingle, a slithering sensation moved up her legs, clawing and seeking for a place to settle. Cold searing pain touched the base of her spine and moved slowly up her back, settling and waiting at her shoulders.

Holding her breath, her mind empty of all thoughts, open and free to be filled with the terrors of the creature yet giving no hook to embed no thought to suckle on, she waited.

Slithering through her it moved down her face, snaking its way through her chest, branching down her arms, seeking, searching for a place to feed. Held in stillness, her eyes open and fixed on the flickering coals of the fire, she closed her vision to what was, and filled it with the darkness of what was not.

Fingers, numb and burning with pain, screamed to find release in movement. Willing herself to stillness, shrouded in sounds prosaic and seductive, she emptied herself of all that was.

Unwilling to shatter the control, Zoloyth watched the blue lines of the creature slither under her skin. Anger, fierce and demanding pulsed with each beat of his heart. Glancing quickly over at the castle, he fixed his eyes on Alathia. Fear gnawed, the balance of all things was challenged, the known was becoming unknown, and uncertainty looked for a place to settle.

Sitting at the roughly hewn table, she rested her hands on the edge and laid her chin on her hands. Looking over at the man opposite her, she waited for him to speak.

"So child, you have wandered from your friends?" She nodded, her eyes wide and holding fear.

"Are you hungry?"

Nodding again she lifted her head and slid her hands under her legs, swinging her feet.

Picking up the small bell that sat on the table he rang it.

"So child, tell me about you," he said gently.

Holding his gaze, she waited, unsure of what to say. Afraid that Celeste would be angry with her, she desperately wanted to leave.

"I should go," she said, wiggling forward on the chair.

"Stay child," he looked up at the man who placed a platter of sweet pastries on the table, "see there is food, eat first then go. You are hungry are you not?"

"Yes," she whispered.

"Good." He took two pastries from the platter and put them on the plate in front of her. "Now eat."

Lifting the pastry, she turned it over and stared at it. The look and feel unfamiliar, she brought it toward her mouth. Biting down, she was surprised by the sweet liquid that filled her mouth and danced on her tongue.

Smiling she took another bite, wiped her hand over her mouth and set the pastry back on the plate.

"I have sent someone to look for your friends," Silias said before biting into a pastry.

"Thank you," she whispered. Looking around the room, she tried to find something that would ease the prickling fear that crawled through her.

"I am a sorcerer… do you know what that is?"

She shook her head and reached for the pastry.

"Would you like to know?" he asked, studying her closely. Shrugging, she bit into the pastry.

"You are not at all interested in finding out?" he asked, surprised by her response.

"Not really," she whispered.

Leaning back in his chair, he folded his arms, a smile creeping slowly over his face.

"I see, well, let me show you," he said, turning to the chair that sat empty next to her. Focusing intently he levitated the chair and moved it across the room.

Following the moving chair, she chewed slowly. Unimpressed, she laid her head on the back of her chair.

"I would like to go now," she said, holding his eyes.

"Would you now?"

"Yes," she whispered.

"So, you didn't think the chair moving by itself was unusual?"

She shrugged and reached for the glass of water on the table.

"No," she took a sip of water and placed the glass back on the table. "Why do that when you can stand and move it quite easily?" she challenged.

Eyes dancing with laughter he shook his head.

"So what would impress you, a dragon perhaps, or lightning falling from the ceiling?"

"No, I've seen a dragon and lightning," she said quietly.

"Oh child you are a strange one," he whispered. "Are you afraid of me?"

Tilting her head slightly, she searched his face before answering.

"No, not afraid."

"What is it then?"

"I don't think you speak the truth."

Unable to hide his surprise at her answer, he rubbed his chin thoughtfully.

"Why do you say that?"

"Because you don't have anyone looking for my friends."

"And you know that how?"

"Your eyes told me what your mouth did not," she said innocently, biting down into the pastry. "What else have my eyes told you?" Chewing thoughtfully, she swallowed and looked over at him.

"Lots of things," she whispered.

"Oh?"

"Thank you for the food," she stood carefully pushing back the chair, "but I need to go."

"Sit," he snapped.

Turning quickly to look at him, she pulled the chair back and sat.

"Now, you are on a quest I believe…there is no need for your quest, you could stay here."

"No I couldn't," she said, "I don't like it here."

"There are lots of people, friends you could make, things you could do," he challenged.

Breathing out slowly she shook her head.

"There is no truth," she whispered.

"What do you mean?" he asked. Intrigued by her responses, he moved his chair closer.

"I can feel it, it is not here," she said softly.

"Well, what does truth feel like?"

Pursing her lips she thought through the question.

"Like a cloak that fits well."

"Tell me more."

"It's snug, it doesn't itch or pull, it keeps the cold out and it feels right to wear," she looked to him for approval.

"So truth is like that?"

She nodded, "I think so yes," she whispered.

"Who told you this?"

Looking down at her plate and the half eaten pastry she shook her head. "No one," she whispered.

oving quickly through the streets they searched for the child.

"Meld with her," Phiobe suggested.

"No, Silias may feel it, become aware of the meld."

"Celeste, that risk you will need to take," he said, scanning the group of children playing in the mud.

Calming her thoughts, she leaned heavily against him.

"I'm not sure I can," she whispered.

"Come," he said gently, sliding his arm around her waist, "rest a little." Leading her to a step he waited until she was seated.

"Stay," she reached for his hand, "please, I don't know that I have anything left to fight if needed."

Settling next to her, resting his hand on her shoulder, he scanned the people moving around them in the hope of seeing the girl.

"Silias is more powerful than I thought," she said softly. "The Council needs to know this."

"They know," he said, turning to look at her. "They keep their knowledge hidden from him, waiting for the time to take that power."

"I trust you speak truth," she whispered. "If he has the child, I fear we may not succeed in taking her back."

"We will do what is necessary, if she so wishes to leave, then we will fight to leave."

"If she chooses to stay?"

He smiled. "She will not, this truth I know," he said quietly. "I have seen in her something I have not seen before. There is something about this one that sets her apart from the others. I know you are tired… reach for her, meld with her, find her."

$\mathcal{S}$winging her legs, she held his eyes, aware of the gentle caress of Celeste reaching for her.

"I hear you," she said connecting with the meld.

"Where are you?"

Reaching for the pastry she bit down. Holding it in front of her mouth she focused her mind on Celeste.

"With Silias."

"Child?" he asked, leaning forward.

Chewing slowly she looked up at him.

"This is nice," she said, biting down on the pastry again.

Smiling, he leaned back, watching her eat.

"Child, reach for me, I need you to search for me," Celeste whispered.

Turning in her chair, she fixed her gaze on the wall behind her. Reaching for Celeste, she pushed deeply, drawing her closer, waiting for the full connection of the meld.

"Well done little one… now look around the room so I may see where you are."

Swinging her legs, she lifted the pastry from the plate, and jumped from the chair. Walking slowly towards the large shelves behind Silias, she turned to look at him.

"What's this?" she asked, reaching for a small ceramic jar which seemed to pulse with life.

"Leave it," he said, standing and moving towards her.

"It's so pretty," she said, looking up at him.

"I know, please don't touch it, it is very rare and extremely precious."

"What's in it?"

"Oil," he said softly.

"Healing oil?" she asked with innocence.

"Yes."

"I see little one," Celeste whispered, "just hold on to me, I will find you."

Touching the rolls of parchment next to the ceramic jar, she focused on Celeste.

"What are these?"

"Sacred writings," he said.

"What makes them sacred?"

"All teaching is sacred when held as truth and revered."

Biting down on the pastry she stood watching him, filling her senses with the room, melding deeply with Celeste.

"Is this where you live?" she asked, walking toward a tapestry hidden behind a large mirror.

"Yes."

Looking in the mirror at him, she tried to focus. Tiredness rested heavily, the strain of hiding the meld taking its toll.

His image shivered in the reflection. Captivated by what she could see, she moved closer to the cold glass.

"Don't, little one," Celeste's voice shattered her compose.

Lowering her hand, she continued to stare at his reflection. The shimmering stroked and caressed, moving freely around him, anchored by an unseen hook. A part of, yet separate.

"So, you see me?" he whispered.

"Yes," she said softly. Her hand moving without thought to touch the mirror.

"Step back little one, step back," Celeste encouraged her.

Moving closer to her, he smiled. The shimmering intensified. Stepping back she breathed out slowly, unaware of his closeness. Fear and unease began to weaken the meld.

"Little one, don't let go," Celeste encouraged.

"He is like the creature." The words meant only for Celeste, escaped through clenched teeth, filling the room.

"Am I?" He laughed, taking another step forward.

"Yes," she whispered.

"Little one we are close, move away from the mirror."

Shaking her head, trying to break from the eyes that held her captive and the shimmering that fascinated, she took a small step to the side. Focusing on the edges of the tapestry she breathed in the colours that dust and neglect could not hide.

$\mathcal{R}$esonating against the wall, the door shuddered with the force that had flung it open.

Phiobe stood, dagger drawn, his face unreadable. Celeste stood beside him, a dagger held tightly in her hand. She glanced quickly at the young girl before moving toward Silias.

"Welcome," he smiled, opening his arms and bending from the waist.

"Come child," Celeste said softly, holding out her hand.

She took a small step toward Celeste.

"Child," encouraged Celeste, motioning her forward with her hand.

"Well now, it looks like you have lost another one," Silias mocked.

Silias grabbed her hand and turned to face Phiobe and Celeste. "It is time for you to leave," he said.

Shaking her hand free she stepped closer to the mirror.

"I am not staying," she whispered.

A smile settling lightly on her lips, Celeste moved closer.

"Then come child," she whispered.

"If I move he will grab me," she said, "his heart is clear to see."

Raising an eyebrow in mock surprise, Silias turned to look at her.

"Such innocence," he scorned. Glancing over at Phiobe he reached for the child.

"Don't," Phiobe hissed, "I will use this," slicing the dagger through the air.

"Oh, I don't think you will."

"Think what you may, truth will be in the action of drawing your blood and watching it spill freely on the floor."

"Stop," the young girl said, "there is no need for this."

"Listen to the child," Silias said, inching his way closer to her.

"Don't come near me," she whispered.

"Oh child, come now," he breathed. "Surely, you know that I would not hurt you."

"So you say," she said softly.

The smile broke freely, Celeste took another step toward Silias.

Turning quickly, he focused on the chair, sliding it across the room and slamming it into Phiobe.

"That was not nice," the child said. Raising her hand, she melded with the table. The plates rattled, the glass of water shattered, the table moved with speed across the room towards Silias.

Turning quickly he held out his hand and forced the table backwards.

"Well I was not expecting that," he laughed.

Flinging the chair aside, Phiobe moved with purpose toward him.

Cautiously Celeste moved towards the child.

Plates flew from the table. Phiobe brushed them aside, unfazed by the splintering ceramic.

"Child, come," Celeste whispered.

"Wait," she replied, holding up her hand.

"Child," Celeste breathed.

"It is not time," she whispered, her eyes on Phiobe.

"Go child," he yelled, lunging at Silias.

Forced back by an unseen hand, Phiobe staggered, grabbing the table for balance.

Holding out her hand the child beckoned Celeste to her. Raising her other hand she focused on the blue ceramic jar. Shuddering under the unseen touch, it lifted slowly from the shelf.

Seeing the movement out of the corner of his eye, Silias screamed. Hand outstretched, he ran to the shimmering jar.

"Phiobe," the child called, holding tightly to Celeste, "run to Celeste."

Releasing her hold on the ceramic jar, she turned to the mirror, pushing it aside with the power of the meld, she revealed the tapestry. Turning, Celeste gasped with surprise at the picture before her.

The golden thread moved quickly, snaking its way through the dust filled image.

  Pulling Celeste toward it, she turned looking for Phiobe. He smiled at her and nodded. Lifting the tapestry from the wall, surprised by its weight and the way it drained her, she pulled it to them with the meld. Feeling the warmth of Phiobe's hand on hers, she smiled. Lifting the tapestry over them she let if fall, melding, the tapestry consumed them.

Wind, gentle and cool caressed her hair and danced playfully with her skirt. Standing atop the mountain she stepped back looking up at the grandeur of what was.

Four winged ones nestled two abreast. The grey yellow of their skin reflected the muted light that surrounded her. Taller than two men, their bodies rippling with strength, their beaks were honed and shaped like that of a trumpet. The tuft of feathers sitting atop their heads danced with the wind. Eyes bright they watched her closely.

She rested her hand gently on the blue shimmering stone. Closing her eyes she sought for understanding, for knowledge of what should be. The massive stone moved effortlessly, beckoning her into a long hallway.

Drinking in the beauty surrounding her, she sighed deeply, each step echoing softly measured by the beating of her heart.

"Welcome," a voice rich and flavoured, holding beauty and power greeted her.

Turning slowly, she looked up at the figure before her. Tall, his skin the richest of browns, his eyes the darkest of blues captured hers.

"Thou art alone?"

"Yes," she whispered.

"That be unusual," he said gently.

"It is what it is," she said quietly.

"Aye," he smiled, "come, they wait for you."

Placing her hand in his she walked silently beside him.

"Thou art afraid?"

"No," she whispered.

"Good there be no need for fear."

"As you say."

"Aye," he chuckled, "we are here. Walk through that door."

Uncurling her hand from his, she moved slowly toward the door. It swung open to reveal a large stone hewn chamber. A marble table sat to the side of the great chamber, a fire burnt fiercely in the centre, the smoke wafting towards a small opening that gave glimpses of the darkening sky. The light from the fire reflected off the polished stone, filling the chamber with a warmth and glow that spoke of comfort and safety.

"Child."

She turned to the voice, captivated by the purity of its tone. Sitting around the marble table, clothed in robes of emerald green, the Ancients waited.

Her eyes on the woman who had summoned her, she sat on the chair that waited for her.

"Welcome," the woman said softly, a smile carrying the word.

"Thank you," she whispered.

"Thou hast undertaken this journey on thy own?"

"Yes."

"Why?"

"It is the way," she whispered.

"Aye, it is the way. Child thy quest begins soon, thou art prepared for such?"

Looking at the six faces that captivated her eyes and calmed the uncertainty that threatened to steal her thoughts, she smiled.

"I think so… I do not know if am prepared."

"Many challenges thou hast faced, from these thou hast learnt of what is?"

"Yes."

"Thou art prepared." The women smiled and leaned back in the chair.

"Child," a male voice broke through her uncertainty.

"Yes," she whispered, holding his eyes.

"Dost thou know who we be?"

"Yes, you are the Ancients, the holders of all things," she said.

"Aye, who did teach thee this truth?"

She shook her head and lowered her eyes.

"No one," she whispered.

"Then how dost thou know this to be so?"

"It is what it is," she said, her voice growing strong with confidence.

A smile broke across his face, settling in eyes sparkling with enjoyment. "Aye. It be such," he said gently. "What dost thou know of the quest?"

"Nothing," she said softly.

"Nothing? Yet thou hast chosen such a journey?"

"Yes."

"Why?" the woman asked.

Tilting her head slightly she looked over at the woman, searching for the words to wrap around the thoughts that filled her mind.
"It is the way," she said softly.
Smiling, the woman leaned forward, resting her hands on the marble top.

"It is the way, what dost that mean to thee?"

"I don't really know," she moved forward in her chair, "I feel it, that is all I know."

"Thou feels it be such?"

She nodded. "Yes, it is what it is, and so it is the way."

"Aye," she whispered, taking time to look at the faces next to her.

"Thou hast questions which need answers?"

"No," the child whispered.

"Dost thou not seek knowledge?"

"Knowledge comes by way of words, understanding by experience, I have learnt there be times when understanding is greater than knowledge," she replied carefully.

"Wisdom thou speaks," said one of the Ancients.

"I think at times knowledge stops us from understanding," she said softly, "I want both."

"I think child thou already hast both," the woman said gently.

"It be unusual for one to sit where thee sits and not to have the many questions," said another.

She shrugged. "I have questions, but to ask them may not be wisdom," she said confidently.

The woman walked to the child. Kneeling down in front of her, she rested her hands on either side of her face, and looked deeply into her eyes.

"Thou dost not seek even the names we wear?" she asked gently.

"No," she whispered, captivated by the face before her, "you would tell me if you wanted me to know."

"Truth thee speaks," she whispered.

Hands warm and comforting cradled the child's head, waves of colour and warmth flooded through her. She placed her hands over the Ancients. The need to connect, to feel fully the gentleness of her touch and the purity of her thought overwhelmed her. A silent tear ran gently down her cheek. Closing her eyes, she surrendered to all that was and all that would be.

Gentle hands lifted her from the chair and carried her to the corner of the chamber, laying her gently on the furs and covering her with another.

lathia breathed deeply. Shaking her hands to ease the pain of stillness, she glanced over at Zoloyth.

"Mistress?"

"I be fine," she whispered.

Moving closer to her, he settled comfortably, searching her body for any signs of poison which may have found a place to settle.

"It did find nothing to feed on," she said quietly.

"It be summoned," he said, looking around the keep, searching for hidden dangers.

"Aye," she breathed. Resting against him, comforted by his strength, the beauty of all that he held, she closed her eyes.

"Mistress," he said softly, enfolding his wings around her.

Breathing deeply, taming the fear and uncertainty, allowing the emotions to freely roam and escape through silent tears, she waited.

The setting sun moved slowly, casting shadows around the keep.

Holding Alathia, Zoloyth watched the shadows grow in length and depth, aware of the battle that raged within her.

Honoured by her trust, humbled by her need, held in stillness in respect for the one he held, he waited.

Two figures walked toward the keep, heads bowed, the slowness of their walk depicting the depth of their perceived loss.

"Mistress," he said gently, "they return."

Alathia moved from his embrace.

"The child be not with them," she whispered.

"Nay," he breathed, fighting the anger that surged.

*E*xamining the child's wrist, the woman gently touched the scar, running her finger over the red cord fused with flesh.

"She hath not complained of this?"

"Nay," she whispered. "I wish to meld with her, to walk as she doth walk, to see as she doth see." She looked up at those standing over the child.

"Wisdom this be not, she will see what thou dost, and walk as thou dost walk," one said.

"She sleeps, this be a time to meld, when there canst be resistance or rebellion," she said quietly.

"What will thee gain from such?"

"Understanding," she smiled.

"Aye, if thou dost believe it must be done, then thee hast the blessing of all... Meld with caution."

"Aye," she breathed, gently holding the child's hand.

Lying next to the girl, pulling the fur over them both, she closed her eyes and focused on the meld.

"Child, child."

Pushing deeply, she searched for a connection.

"Child, this be Ileana," she said gently, reaching to connect.

"I hear you," the child whispered.

"There be no need for fear, look to me little one, and see that thou knows me."

Tossing restlessly, the young girl fought the connection.

"Little one, be at peace, there is naught to fear," she said gently.

Moving closer in the meld, she reached for the outstretched hand.

"Well done child... let thy body rest, calm thy thoughts, no harm will come to thee."

Breathing deeply she moved closer to Ileana.

"I am very tired," she whispered.

"Aye, the day has been long and thou hast seen much."

"Yes."

"Come little one, I wish to walk with thee."

"Where are we going?"

"Trust," she squeezed her hand gently, "allow the meld, follow my lead, no harm will come to thee."

*W*ater lapped gently at her feet. Moving them slowly, she smiled at the ripples that swirled with precision. Leaning back on her hands, she looked up at the small lights scattered over the roof of the cave.

"How did you know about this place," she whispered, turning to look at Ileana.

"We are melded little one, I know thy thoughts as thee doth know mine," she said gently.

"I think Celeste is going to be angry with me."

"Why doth thou believe this?"

Sighing, she moved her feet quickly in the water.

"I didn't tell her what I was doing, she won't know where I am."

Ileana sat quietly, connecting deeply, waiting for the child to find a place of calmness.

"How did thee travel to the mount of the Ancients?"

"It was the tapestry," she whispered, turning to look at her. "I saw it, and so I thought to be here."

"And of Celeste?"

"I thought her to go to the keep," she said shyly.

Ileana smiled: "So thy thought was to come alone?"

"Yes."

"Why?"

"It seemed to be the way," she whispered.

Resting her hand on the girls' shoulder, she smiled.

"The way hast been that Celeste brings all here," she said gently, "but I see thy heart hast understanding that perchance others have not."

"She will be angry."

"Nay, she will be worried, but wrath she will not hold."

"I hope so," she said quietly.

"Child, it be time for thee to have greater understanding, say to me what thou knows of the Ancients."

Breathing deeply, she closed her eyes.

"You are an Ancient," she said cautiously, "you know all things."

"This be truth all do know. What truth doth thee to know?"

"That you are," she whispered, opening her eyes and looking into Ileana's.

"Aye," she rested her hand on the child's head. "Little one, thou must choose a name for self."

"Why?"

"It be important to do so," she said gently. "Child, a name chosen for self dost give thee a sense of being. Truth it be that other names be chosen for thee, but the name thee chooses be the one that is thine alone."

"Why can't another chose?" the child asked. Resting her hands on her lap, she touched her scared wrist, tugging at the strip of cloth that bound it tightly.

"They will, many names may be given to thee on the quest. Child, the name thou chooses none doth need to know. It be the name that reminds thee of all that is, and all thou art. It is the one thy heart holds as a keepsake and none can take from thee."

Searching through the words, looking for their meaning, she pursed her lips, tilted her head and looked over at Ileana.

"Child, I hear thy confusion, let the words settle."

"So it is only important to me?"

"Aye. As thee walks the quest, thou wilt be named based on the thread thou weaves. Named as others do see thee, how thee sees self be far greater than any name given by another."

"So I am like the thread in the tapestry?"

"Aye, thee weaves a tapestry on thy quest. What thee weaves others will see."

"And if I choose to end the quest?"

"That choice be thine. Thy thread will no longer weave; perchance another will see and weave next to thine so thy quest be complete.

Child, on thy quest the thread can be woven in many ways into thy tapestry. Some will see beauty in thy weave, others will see dimly. Some will be blinded. Yet thee continues the quest, holding to the name thou hast chosen."

"Of the tapestries in the castle, Zoloyth said that they were not mine to create," she said softly.

"Aye, that is truth."

"I don't understand," she whispered.

"Little one, when a tapestry is woven all threads are secure. Thy eyes may not like what be seen, thy heart may not dance with joy. Yet, it is woven… Perchance thy thread can be added to a tapestry if the thread be needed. If not, then thy hand does not create, nor does thy heart desire to gaze upon. This is when thee steps away and continues on the quest that is thine."

*F*lames from the fire cast shadows over the small group, each lost in thought and focused on the meal before them.

"Power she did use against Silias?" Alathia asked, breaking the silence.

"Yes, she can meld and move with thoughts," Celeste replied, dipping the bread into the broth on her plate.

"Thinkest thou she melded with Silias for such power?"

"I don't know, I know it was not with me."

"Perchance she be more aware of what is, than we did know," Alathia mused.

"She has wisdom, she sees more than others," Phiobe said quietly.

"That is truth," Zoloyth said thoughtfully. "Powers she has, powers she used. Perchance her powers are protecting her now."

"Master, I failed in bringing her back safely," Phiobe stood slowly, "of this I am truly pained."

"None did fail," Alathia said sharply, "it is what it is. She did pull thee both into the tapestry and direct thy path. We must believe the path she chose for self is the one she must be on."

Laying her plate on the ground, Celeste moved her stool closer to the fire.

"I have tried to meld with, to reach for her. I cannot, the meld is blocked."

"That can only mean that she is with the Ancients," Zoloyth stated.

"Aye, and so we wait."

$\mathcal{S}$tretching slowly, pushing back the furs, she looked around her. The fire continued to burn fiercely as it had done since the beginning of all things.

"Thou art awake little one," Ileana said gently, moving away from the fire towards the bed.

"Yes," she said shyly.

"Come, we eat, then I have much to show you." Holding out her hand she waited for the child.

"Little one thou art troubled?"

Nodding, she sat on the bed swinging her legs, her hands tucked under her.

Ileana rested her hand gently on her shoulder. "What troubles thee?"

"All this," she whispered.

"Find the words, tell me thy heart and all that brings such sorrow."

The fear that had bubbled since the meld, escaped in tears, falling silently and without restraint.

"Oh child," she breathed, pulling her close. Melding gently, she pushed past the fear and searched for the words unable to be spoken. Resisting the intrusion, the child tried to block the meld, walling her thoughts, surrounding them with emotion that found release in tears.

"I see thy fear, I hear thy cry for understanding. Aloneness thou fears, to hold thy name and none doth speak it."

The words spoken in the meld, cut deeply, the walls crumbling, fear freed from restraint clearly seen.

"Yes," she whispered.

"Aye. Child, thy fear be without foundation. Thou hast created without knowledge or understanding of what will be, fearing what could be. Thou hast woven a thread into a tapestry that hath not been sketched."

"What if it's true?" she whispered.

"Thou wishes to make it truth?"

"No."

"Then it shall not be truth for thee. Little one, on the quest thou art equipped with all that is needed. Only when thy heart is filled with doubt, and thy eyes locked onto all that assails thee, dost thou forget what hast been given to thee."

Sighing deeply, her head resting against Ileana, toying with the words spoken, she searched for their meaning.

"So it may not be?"

"Aye, it may not be. Perchance that thee finds thyself in such a place, change the weave. Choosing thy name is the key little one, it doth to anchor thee to self."

"A name is just a name," she whispered.

"Look to me… thee fights the meld, holding words that cause thee pain… The name I speak of doth not be the one that thee speaks when greeting another…. What I speak of is the name that holds all of thee, thy purpose, thy direction, thy dreams. It be the core of thyself. Think of Silias, he greeted thee with the name of sorcerer. Phiobe, as healer and servant… Understanding begins little one?"

"Yes."

"Aye," she kissed the top of her head, "understanding begins to settle in thee."

"I don't know my name," she whispered.

"It dost bubble within thee, a flicker in thy mind, a thought far reached. Do not force the thought, or dig in places where it could hide. Let it come to thee, when it is time, it will be clear."

"What if I never know?"

"Oh, thou wilt know little one. It will whisper to thee, it will direct thy path even if thou hast not heard the whisper. It will strengthen thee, comfort and guide."

"How can that be?"

"It *is*. That is all thee needs to dwell on. Little one, thy name be not a word only to be spoken lightly. It is what defines thee. I ask this, when thee hears the name wind, what thinkest thou?"

Holding the question, she worked through her thoughts.

"It is something you can't see, but you can see where it has been… it can be gentle and fierce, hot and cold," the child replied with care.

"Aye it can be all that and more. It be named wind, yet it is much, showing self in many ways. Those ways can be named storm, or gentle breeze. Yet it still be what it is named, it still be wind. Dost thou begin to understand?" "I think so," she whispered.

"Tell me thy understanding. I do sense it, yet thy words I would hear."

Sighing deeply she moved closer to Ileana, leaning heavily both in the meld and in the body, drawing from her the knowledge, the balance of understanding needed.

"My name tells me what I am," she paused, waiting for acknowledgement.

"Aye little one, and?"

"And it holds my purpose on the quest. It says to me, this is what you are, what you do. But like the wind it can be gentle or fierce."

"Aye," she breathed, stroking the child's head gently.

"The wind changes because the seasons change, so it becomes what it must become in that season. So if I am named, like the wind, I change with the seasons, but I am still what I am named."

"Truth thee speaks little one," she whispered.

"So, choosing my name has already been done, like the wind, it is and was and will be. So it is the same for me on the quest," she said, growing in confidence and understanding, and drawing from the meld the knowledge held by the Ancient.

"Aye."

"You can't hold the wind, or stop it from being wind. It can be directed and blocked by a shelter, but the wind still is."

"Truth, little one," she said gently.

"If I am like the wind, my fierceness can blow the shelter down, so I keep moving on my path, or go around it, yet I still am, my name has not changed. Who I am is still what I am named."

"Aye."

"So I can be shaped, harnessed and put to use; but I am still who I am named. My purpose does not change."

"Aye little one, understanding thee begins to have. The wind cannot become snow, yet it can move the snow and carry it. It cannot become water, yet it can move the water and carry it. Thee cannot become what thou art not, but thee can carry others, weave alongside their thread, give to the tapestry that be woven, all within the purpose of thy name. If the wind did try to become what it is not, well little one, it be not possible for it to do such a thing."

"Even if it wanted to," she stated quietly.

"Aye, even if it should choose to be snow, it cannot be such. Trying would be futile."

"Yes," she breathed.

"So it is with thee little one."

"I think I understand," she whispered.

"Thee did fear none would speak thy name," she said gently.

"Yes," she breathed.

"Of the wind, it cannot be what it be without another. It doth need the flesh of one to feel its touch, to know of its coolness and gentleness.

It doth need the eyes of another to see its fierceness. It doth need the land around it to be formed, the seasons to change to become what it becomes in that season. It can never just to be without another....it be the same for thee little one.

There will be those who weave closely to thee, those who will sense thy touch, know thy hand, have understanding of thy actions and words...never alone shalt thou be."

She waited, letting the words settle.

"If thou chooses aloneness, then thy name will not be heard, thy purpose will be unseen, none will know of thy caress, as it is with the wind. That fear, if held deeply will hide thy name, taking from it the life within."

*T*he four winged ones circled the keep. Resting comfortably the young girl breathed deeply, laying her head against the long neck.

Moving quickly from the shelter, Alathia shaded her eyes with her hand.

"Celeste," she called, "come hither with speed."

Landing gently, the winged one pressed into the ground and waited for her to alight.

"Thank you," she whispered, stroking him gently.

"Child," Alathia called, gathering her skirt and running towards her.

Moving away from the winged one, she walked slowly toward Alathia.

"Child," she breathed, reaching for her hand.

Taking her hand, the child knelt and bowed her head.

"Alathia, keeper of the keep, holder of truth, I greet thee."

"Child," she breathed with surprise.

"I am Chloe, seeker of the quest, I request shelter and succour," she said, lifting her head and holding her eyes.

"I grant thee thy request, my keep be thine, my shelter thy shelter, my people thy people, all that be mine with joy I share with thee," Alathia replied, tempering the surprise from her voice.

"I have naught to give thee in return. I offer my gratitude and respect for what be thine."

"Such payment is more than enough," Alathia said quietly.

"Thank thee," she said quietly.

"Come little one."

Standing slowly, she stood beside Alathia. Sliding her arm around her shoulders, Alathia breathed deeply, knowing the time to leave the keep was close.

"Child," Celeste said, running to them.

Moving away from Alathia, Chloe waited.

"Oh child," Celeste breathed, hugging her tightly.

Stepping back, Chloe knelt, reaching for her hand.

"Greetings Celeste, teacher of all that is truth, holder of those who seek the quest," she said quietly.

"Greetings," she breathed, kneeling and trying to hide her surprise at the formality being shown.

"I am Chloe seeker of the quest, I am welcomed to the keep by the holder of truth. Naught I bring thee. My heart to learn, thy instruction I take, this be what I offer thee."

"Such payment is more than enough," Celeste whispered.

"Thank thee," she whispered.

"Oh, little one," she breathed, pulling her close and holding her tightly. "Much growth since I last saw you."

"Yes," she whispered, falling into Celeste, taking comfort from her touch.

"Come," Celeste said quietly, taking her hand and standing slowly, "Phiobe will be glad to see the."

Smiling, Chloe stood beside her, holding out her hand for Alathia. Together they walked towards the fire, each lost in thought, knowing their time be short.

"Child," Phiobe cried with delight, standing quickly he moved to her. "Little one, I am so glad to see you."

"And I you," she said reaching for his hand.

"You are safe, I have been greatly troubled for you."

"I am safe," she whispered.

"This I see, Zoloyth will be delighted to see you."

"Yes," she smiled. "Thank thee for thy protection, for thy care of all that be of Zoloyth."

Looking over her shoulder at Alathia, he raised his eyebrow, unsure of the change he sensed in the child.

Alathia nodded and smiled, her eyes answering the question he was reluctant to speak.

"Sit little one, and tell us all that has happened," Celeste said, pulling the stools closer to the fire.

Sitting slowly, Chloe stared into the fire, her mind tumbled with thoughts, emotions creeping to the surface.

"I went to the Mount of the Ancients," she said softly, "and was instructed by Ileana."

Celeste turned towards Alathia and held her gaze, melding together, they spoke quietly.

"Mother, what is happening?"

"I do not know, none has been instructed by only one of the Ancients. Two suns have risen, and now she doth return, a child, but not so."

"The quest begins soon," Celeste said in the meld.

"Aye it does."

Turning to face them, Chloe smiled: "Yes, the quest begins soon," she confirmed.

Surprise settled on Alathia's face, untamed and unfettered, moving quickly through her body.

"I hear you both," she melded softly, "I also see your confusion and questions."

"Aye," Celeste breathed.

"It is what it is," Chloe said quietly.

A humming sound filled the silence. Zoloyth circled the keep, his shadow covering all. Settling gently, he moved to Chloe.

"Back I see," he smiled.

"Yes." Kneeling, she touched his talon gently. "I greet thee, protector and healer. I am Chloe, ready for the quest, naught I bring to thee. I offer my heart to hear thy instructions, my respect for thy greatness, this I offer thee," she said quietly.

"Such that thou gives be more than enough."

"Thank thee," she whispered.

"Child, stand," he said gently, "thou hast grown much in the time of instruction."

"I pray this is truth," she answered.

"It is truth," he smiled.

"Aye," Alathia whispered. "Child, sit, tell us of thy heart of all that is." Moving slowly to the stool, she sat, resting her hands in her lap.

"Many things I was shown," she said thoughtfully.

"I did not fail," Phiobe breathed, stirring the pot of broth that sat on the firestones.

"Why did you think that?" the child challenged.

Shaking his head, he sat slowly.

"When we were sent here, I did not know where you were. I was afraid for you, unsure of what was."

"Oh," she breathed, "so you did not see the tapestry as it was?"

He looked up in surprise: "No, I saw nothing."

"Then your eyes were not opened to see," she said gently.

Covering her mouth to hide the smile, Alathia moved her stool closer to the child.

"What doth thou mean?"

"Phiobe knows," she said quietly.

Zoloyth roared with laughter. "The child teaches thee now Phiobe." "It would seem so," he smiled.

"Instruct him child," Zoloyth said.

Turning to look at Zoloyth, she held his gaze, and then turned to Phiobe.

"Maybe all you could see was Silias and all that he did. In seeing only him, your eyes were closed to the tapestry. Even when it fell on you, you did not see."

Pulling his cloak around him, he leaned toward the fire.

"It is like the fire you see now. You have knowledge of what fire does, unless you truly see, you will not see what it does. You can know that it burns, but until you feel the sting of the burn you have no understanding.

You can know that it will heat the broth. Unless you put the broth on to the firestones and watch it change from cool to hot, you have no understanding. You may know it needs wood to feed its hunger, unless you give it what is needs, you have no understanding of how hungry it is," she paused looking to Alathia, hoping her words were truth.

Alathia nodded, reaching for her hand and holding it tightly. Resting her head against Alathia, she closed her eyes, her body tired, her mind filled with things not quite understood. Breathing deeply, she released them, taking comfort in the arms that held her.

"So it was with Silias, you knew of his magic, of what he could do. It was when you felt it, that you had understanding. In that moment your vision became dulled to everything else, you were consumed with the understanding. So the tapestry was not seen, its meaning not understood."

"The child speaks truth," Alathia said gently. "It be in the understanding that we do have vision only for that moment. How can one say they know the sorrow of another, unless consumed by sorrow they have been. When that doth be such, all that can be seen is the sorrow, the eyes be not opened to see aught else.

Such be the way of understanding. When thou doth take the knowledge and understanding and meld as one, then thy eyes can see more than what be."

"It is in that melding the thread breathes, and the weaving continues," Celeste said quietly.

Wrapped in silence, the words settled, each taking what was needed and making it truth.

"She sleeps I think," Phiobe said, breaking the silence that the words had created.

"She sleeps," Zoloyth conformed.

Standing slowly, Phiobe gently lifted her into his arms and carried her to the shelter.

"The child is ready, on the morrow the quest begins," Alathia said quietly.

Standing in the inner room of the castle, surrounded by cedar lined walls, they stood in silence. Looking around her, Chloe gazed upon the timbers, breathing in their strength, the perfume of the wood, the beauty of colour.

"It is time," Celeste said gently.

"Yes," the child breathed.

"Come." Celeste held out her arms to her. Melding with Chloe she spoke of peace and strength, of beauty and honour.

"I understand," the child whispered.

Stepping back, Celeste held her eyes: "Walk the quest with strength little one," she whispered.

Alathia moved forward, beckoning the child to her. Melting in her arms, Chloe held tightly, the tears close, sorrow beginning to settle.

"Little one, all thou needs thou has. Walk the quest in that knowledge, know thy heart, know thy name, and know thy weave will be strong."

Kissing her cheek gently she stood back, her hands resting on the child's shoulders, their eyes locked, aware the child was melding, she waited.

"Thank you," she whispered, "I know this is the way, yet I am sad."

"Aye, child, sorrow doth at times be part of what is. We are never far from thee. In thy heart thou holds all… rest in that."

Stepping back Alathia stood next to Celeste and laid her head on her shoulder. Zoloyth knelt before the child.

"Little one, remember all that has been shown. Trust what you have learned, walk the quest in that knowledge and understanding."

She nodded. Wrapping his wings around her, he held her to him. A tear fell silently, glistening on the emerald scales of his wings.

His hand on the cedar door, Phiobe waited.

"When you are ready little one," he said gently.

"Thank you," she said smiling up at Phiobe. "I will not be a fish."

Laughing, he winked at her: "No I think not. Walk the quest well little one, knowing we know the weave and the strength of your thread."

"It begins," she whispered, stepping through the open door.

Kneeling down, Celeste broke the red cord that tethered them together. A tear furrowing her cheek, the ends of the broken cord fell to the wooden floor.

Darkness surrounded her, she moved quickly, ignoring the pain, eager to commence the quest that was hers.

Pushing against hands that held her tightly, she laid her head against the chest of the one closest, drawing comfort from the beating heart of the one she would call mother.

the Weaving

"This be the beginning, the weaving of what is, the touch of what is to come."

www.ingramcontent.com/pod-product-compliance
Lightning Source LLC
Chambersburg PA
CBHW070334120726
47909CB00008B/2691